Playing by Heart

BY DEBORAH RANEY

ISBN 1-58660-491-0

For more information about Deborah Raney, please access the author's web site at the following Internet address: www.deborahraney.com

Acquisitions and Editorial Director: Rebecca Germany
Editorial Consultant: Becky Durost Fish
Art Director: Robyn Martins
Layout Design: Anita Cook

Published by Barbour Publishing, Inc., P.O. Box 719, Uhrichsville, OH 44683, www.barbourbooks.com

Printed in the United States of America.

5 4 3 2 1

To Ryan and Tobi Layton
Happy second anniversary,
And wishing you many, many more.

I would like to express my deep appreciation to the following people for the roles they played in making this book a reality:

Tammy Alexander and Jill Eileen Smith, for going over the manuscript with a fine-tooth comb and the eagle eyes of gifted writers and editors. Thank you for contributing incredible ideas and insight and for feeding and encouraging my writer's heart. Thank you, Tammy, for coming up with the perfect ending.

Debbie Allen, Lorie Battershill, Terry Stucky, and Max and Winifred Teeter for reading the manuscript in its early stages and offering encouragement and advice.

My editors at Barbour Publishing, Rebecca Germany and Becky Durost Fish.

Dan and Jeanne Billings, owners of the Emma Creek Inn, Hesston, Kansas, for providing the lovely writing retreat that inspired this story. And special thanks to the inn's original Alex, who inspired Art and Maddie's feline friend.

And as always, my precious family for always being there for me. I love you guys with all my heart.

One

Glancing at the chaos around her, Madeleine Houser set her coffee mug on the dining room table and heaved a sigh as she tried to shove another packing carton out of her path. It didn't budge. She bent over and squinted, attempting to read the smudged label penned in her barely legible handwriting. *Kitchen—good china.* Oh. Good thing she'd resisted the temptation to kick the box.

Her gaze traveled to the kitchen. The cupboards gaped open, hinges naked, doors lined up on the floor against the wall in the empty breakfast nook. Even after four days, the smell of wet enamel stung her nostrils. The cabinetry wore three smooth coats of Winter Bisque semigloss, but the flooring couldn't be laid until the electrician fixed the mess he'd made of the wiring. And she didn't dare put her china in the cupboards until all that was done.

What had her sister gotten her into? Kate's husband

had been transferred to Ohio, but with Kate and Maddie's mother in the nursing home here in Clayton, Kate had begged Maddie to leave her beloved New York loft and move into Kate and Jed's house on Harper Street while it was being refurbished to sell. "You can write anywhere, Maddie. Besides, the rent isn't half what you're paying for that loft," Kate had pled in the big-sister voice that, even as a grown woman of thirty-four, Maddie couldn't seem to resist. So here she was in Clayton, Kansas—the middle of nowhere—proving quite soundly that one could not write just *anywhere*.

With a long sigh, Maddie lugged the carton of china out of the way and pushed it against the dining room wall to join half a dozen other derelict boxes. Retrieving her mug from the table, she wove her way through the maze to the kitchen, poured herself another cup of coffee, and took it back to the dining room. She blew a long strand of dish-water blond hair out of her eyes and sat down at the table. In the midst of the piles of books and packing boxes and unsorted mail strewn across the table, her laptop computer glared accusingly at her.

Ignoring the disorder, she pulled the computer close, pushed her glasses up on her nose, and tried to remember where she'd left off. Ah, yes. The heartless landlord had just evicted the young widow. *Oh, brother, Houser, how cliché can you get?* Well, tough. She didn't have time to change the whole plot now. She'd written almost two thousand words this morning, but given her track record lately, she'd be lucky if fifty of them were worth keeping.

For the hundredth time, Maddie wondered what she'd been thinking when she'd allowed her editor to talk her into a January 1 deadline in the middle of this cross-country move. "You can do it, Madeleine," Janice had crooned in her conniving editor's voice. "If we can get this book on the shelves before next Christmas, the first print run will sell out in a month. Come on. Say you'll do it. Houser fans are clamoring for your next book. Please?"

Over the six years she'd been Maddie's editor, Janice Hudson had become a dear friend, but right now Maddie wanted to strangle her. She did not write well under pressure. And she was just about at her limit in that department.

Maddie edited the sentence in front of the blinking cursor. Absently reaching for her coffee, she took a sip and promptly burned the tip of her tongue. Biting back a scream, she forced herself to return to the nineteenth century and the plight of Anne Caraway, her suffering heroine. Poor Anne. First she'd lost her dearly loved William, and now she was being evicted from her home. Her favorite heroine was alone with a small child to care for, and now Maddie was about to throw Anne onto the mean streets of Chicago. It was the bane of an author—to make her beloved characters suffer immeasurable sorrow, to put them in the furnace and then turn up the fire. But one had no story without conflict, and conflict often equaled sorrow. So onto the streets Anne Caraway and little Charlie must go. Maddie typed furiously.

The faint echo of dripping water pierced her concentration, causing her fingers to still. She glanced up from her laptop and tilted her head to one side, listening. Hmmm. Was it raining? Who could tell with the heavy drapes that covered the dining room's high windows? Those would have to go. But first she had to finish this book. Brushing off the temptation to get up and check outside, she turned back to the keyboard. She typed twenty words before the *drip, drip, drip* became demanding.

She pushed her chair back and navigated the labyrinth of cardboard boxes toward the sound of the water. It seemed to be coming from the kitchen. Dodging sawhorses the contractors had left and appliances that had been pulled away from the walls, she followed the annoying sound across the kitchen to the basement door. As a rule, basements gave her the creeps; but in this tornado alley on the Kansas prairie, it was a rare house that didn't have one. She'd been relieved that Kate and Jed's charming Tudor had only a closet-sized cellar. Just enough space to provide refuge from a cyclone, but not enough to have dark, dank corners where. . .well, where whatever it was she was afraid of could hide.

Maddie opened the door and gasped. The wooden steps at the bottom of the flight glistened with water; and from the far end of the cellar, she could hear the unmistakable sound of water trickling into more water.

She glanced up at the naked lightbulb hanging over the stairs. *Rats!* The string attached to the pull chain was caught on one of the splintered rafters overhead. Maddie straddled the steps, one foot on the top landing, the other on the thin ledge that ran the length of the stairwell. Grabbing the door handle for support, she scooted along the ledge, grasping blindly for the string. She gasped as she lost her balance, inadvertently pushing the door shut behind her.

The stairwell went dark. Miraculously she found the string with the next random swing of her arm. Not so miraculously when she pulled on the chain, the light flickered, then sparked. Next Maddie heard the ominous sound of every electric device in the house powering down. She barely had time to wonder if she'd remembered to save her work to the computer's hard drive when she slipped off the ledge. A sharp pain sliced through her left ankle, and she bumped down half the flight of stairs.

When the stairwell quit spinning and she could figure out which way was up, she crawled back up to the kitchen, opened the door, and pulled herself to her feet. *Ouch!* Her ankle had already swollen to the size of a small grapefruit, and it hurt to put any weight on it. But her first concern was the electricity. Damp and aching, she hobbled to the cordless phone on the kitchen wall. Dead. Thankfully the phone in the dining room had a dial tone. She rummaged through the desk drawer until she found the thin phone book. Flipping to the *R*s, she found the number of her neighbor, Ginny Ross. Ginny answered on the second ring.

"Ginny? Hi, it's Madeleine Houser next door. Is your electricity out?"

"No. Well, at least I don't believe so. Just a minute. . ."

Maddie heard an oven door creak open and then what sounded like the ding of a microwave. "No. Everything's still on over here."

"Rats! I think I've blown another fuse. And there's water in the—ouch!"

"Madeleine? What's happened? Are you all right?"

Maddie cringed as she eased into the desk chair. "I'm fine. I fell down the stairs and sprained my ankle."

"My, you scared me. I thought you'd electrocuted yourself."

Maddie gave a humorless laugh. "Nothing so dramatic, I'm afraid. Sorry to bother you. I just didn't want to call the electrician again if it was only—"

"I'll be right over."

The phone went dead, and Maddie sat for a few seconds, staring at the receiver, before she realized that Ginny meant her words literally. Maddie had only met Ginny Ross two weeks ago, but already she'd grown to love the woman. At eighty-four, Ginny epitomized the word *spry*. Widowed for a quarter of a century, her neighbor was as independent and modern as any of Maddie's cultured, thirty-something

New York friends. With Maddie's own mother's mind ravaged by Alzheimer's disease, it was good to have a wise, older woman to talk to.

"Yoo-hoo!" Ginny's cheery voice floated from the back mudroom.

"Come on in, Ginny. But watch your step."

Ginny bustled through the mudroom and into the kitchen, weaving her way through the chaos to Maddie's side. "Now what did you do to yourself?" She bent to inspect Maddie's swollen ankle. "Oh, my! Are you sure you didn't break it?"

"I don't think so," Maddie told her, rubbing the tender area around the swelling.

Ginny scooted another chair in front of Maddie and helped her elevate her foot. Then she went to the freezer and rummaged inside until she unearthed a package of frozen peas. "Here we go." She wrapped the icy bag in a dishcloth and draped it gently over Maddie's ankle, then glanced around the kitchen. "This place is a mess! How are you ever going to finish that book in this shambles?"

Maddie couldn't help it. The tears that had been pent up for weeks overflowed. "Oh, Ginny, I don't know. I'm already so far behind I can't imagine how I'll make my deadline. And if I don't have electricity, I'm sunk."

"Well, of course you are," Ginny said, making sympathetic clucking noises with her tongue. She surveyed the kitchen again. "This will never do. I'd offer to let you write at my house, but I'm afraid my beginning piano students would make this wreck seem like a haven of peace."

Maddie swiped at a tear and forced a smile. "I appreciate that, Ginny. But it's not your problem. I'll figure something out. Maybe I can just go to the library. . . ."

"Are you kidding? You'd have a constant stream of onlookers gawking and pestering you with questions." Ginny snapped her fingers and turned to Maddie with a triumphant gleam in her eyes. "I know just the place. My friend Arthur Tyler has that monstrous house sitting empty ever since his Annabeth died. They had a booming bed-and-breakfast until Annabeth's health got so bad. Arthur rarely has guests now, but I know he wouldn't mind if you went there to write. You probably wouldn't want to stay overnight. I don't think that man would know a dust rag or a home-cooked breakfast if they jumped up and bit him—that was always Annabeth's department. But he wouldn't mind if you used one of the rooms. Arthur is a professor at the university. Keeps saying he's going to retire but never does. Well, what do you think, Madeleine?"

Dizzy from Ginny's spiel, Maddie wasn't sure about the idea at all. But she had to do something. She certainly wasn't going to get her book finished here. "Where is this place, Ginny?"

"It's just a couple miles outside of town. Out on Hampton Road. Pretty little place. Peaceful. Annabeth's parents ran the inn for years. Named it after her, of course.

Grover and I stayed there for our fortieth anniversary. Seemed kind of silly to stay overnight two miles from home, but it was nice. Kind of romantic. . ." A faraway look came to Ginny's eyes, and an ever-so-faint blush touched her powdered cheeks. "Let me give Arthur a call," she said, suddenly turning her attention back to Maddie. "You just get the plumber and electrician here, and I'll take care of everything else."

two

The inn was beautiful. Sunlight splashed saffron patches on the shiny wood floors and caused the jewel tones in the window coverings and upholstery to glow. In spite of her injured ankle, Madeleine felt better just standing in the spacious parlor, looking into rooms that were tidy and free of packing crates.

"Arthur said to tell you to make yourself at home," Ginny said, dropping a key ring into the pocket of her bulky sweater and running a hand absently over the mantle. Her fingertips left a trail in the fine film of dust. She clucked her tongue and shook her gray head. "Annabeth always kept this place spotless. Even after she got so sick. Poor Arthur. . . ."

"Was Annabeth a friend of yours?" Maddie asked.

"She was. A dear friend. She and Arthur both. It was a terrible thing, her dying." Ginny picked up a heavy pewter candlestick from the mantle and wiped the dust away with the sleeve of her sweater.

"I'm so sorry. . . ."

Ginny nodded slowly, then gave a resolute bob of her chin and brightened. "I'd show you the rest of the house, but I don't think your ankle would appreciate that steep staircase yet. Arthur said you could set up shop in one of the guest rooms, but he doesn't use any of the house proper—he lives in the apartment on the lower level—so I'm sure you can use the main living area here if you prefer. Or you could hole up in this bedroom. It's the only guest room on the main floor." Ginny opened the wide French doors off the living room to reveal a guest room beautifully decorated with dark Old English antiques. "By the way, the only rest room on the first floor is in here."

Maddie poked her head into the room and took in the modern pedestal sink on the far wall just outside a door that apparently concealed the bath.

Ginny pulled the doors closed and led the way through a wide arched doorway into the dining room. To the left, an open staircase led down, Maddie presumed, to the apartment where the proprietor lived. The steep stairway was defended by an oak railing; and in the middle of the room, a huge, round, antique oak table sat on an Oriental rug. The walls wore old-fashioned wallpaper in lovely shades of plum and burnished gold, and the room was furnished with a fine antique buffet with silver tea service and two drop-leaf tables that bore baskets of teas and jams. An open doorway led to a small galley kitchen, where an array of dishes and baskets and jars of canned goods were displayed on open shelving.

"You're sure Mr. Tyler won't care if I set up right here?" Maddie tipped her head toward the dining room table.

"I'd say this is perfect," Ginny said, obviously pleased with herself. "I'll leave now so you can get to work."

"Oh, Ginny, it *is* perfect. How can I ever thank you?"

Ginny winked. "Just finish that book, Sweetie. I've only about three chapters before I finish my last Houser novel, and then I'm fresh out of reading material."

Ginny bustled out the front door, and Maddie was left in the blessed quiet of the old house. She took her laptop from its case and set it on the table, positioning her chair so that she had a lovely view through the arched doorway all the way to the front hall. She connected the power adaptor and plugged it into an outlet.

Remembering the sack lunch and coffee she'd brought, she took them out of her bag and hobbled into the kitchen with them. She opened the refrigerator. The shelves were empty save for a few cans of soda and a package of ground coffee. Maddie put the lunch bag on the middle shelf, feeling strangely as though she were trespassing. But Ginny had said that Arthur Tyler insisted she have free run of the place, including full use of the kitchen. Turning, Maddie surveyed the rest of the room. A half-dozen mismatched coffee cups and saucers sat in the sink. A decrepit coffeemaker sat on the counter with an inch of cold, dark brew in the bottom of the carafe. She dumped the old grounds, rinsed the pot, and found fresh filters in a drawer under the counter. Once the coffee was brewing, Maddie went back to the dining room and finished setting up shop. She unloaded her bag, placing her dictionary and several reference books to her left, her notebook and pen to her right.

She popped a Mozart CD into her computer. Classical music filled the room, and Maddie sighed as she sank into the brocade padded chair, slipped off her shoes, and propped her swollen ankle on the seat of a neighboring chair. The timeless melody, the rich aroma of fresh coffee, and her Victorian surroundings transported her back in time; and as she put her fingers to the keyboard, the words flowed as they hadn't in months. *I don't know you, Arthur Tyler, but God bless your generous old heart.*

For the next two hours, Maddie typed, getting up only to refill her coffee mug. Her plot was moving along nicely when a polite "meow" caused her to look up from her computer screen.

A monstrous gray-and-white cat stuck its head through the balusters and peered at her. Coming up the last step, the cat sashayed over to Maddie, arched its back, and rubbed against her ankle before plopping down on her right foot.

Maddie took off her glasses and laid them on the table. "Well, hello there, Kitty," she said, reaching down to stroke the leonine head. "They didn't tell me about you."

The cat purred in response and nestled closer to Maddie. Though the house didn't have the chill she'd expected of a high-ceilinged Victorian, the cat's warmth was welcome. The old schoolhouse clock on the wall over the stairwell ticked a reassuring cadence, and she wrote for another hour while the cat napped. The clock's muffled chime and the growl of her own stomach brought Maddie out of Anne Caraway's world and back to the present. Wiggling her toes and lowering her left foot from its elevated position on the other chair, she nudged the cat. "Sorry, Kitty, but I need to get up and stretch a bit."

The cat yawned, bowed his back, and gave a short, friendly "mew" before following her into the kitchen. Maddie took her lunch from the refrigerator and ate it, leaning against the kitchen counter, her mind still on her story. Though her ankle throbbed, it felt good to stand up and flex her muscles a bit. After she finished her sandwich, she filled the sink with warm, sudsy water and washed the dishes, putting them to drain on the old-fashioned wire dish rack. She'd forgotten how nice it was to be in an operational kitchen, and she spent a few extra minutes wiping the countertops and washing smudges from the refrigerator door.

With the kitchen tidy, she went back to her computer and set to work. Her feline friend had disappeared. She heard the clock chime the half hour and looked up, surprised that it was two-thirty already. Checking her word count, she was thrilled to discover that she'd written almost three thousand words since morning. A few more days like this and she might actually believe she could make her deadline. She saved the file, closed her laptop, and began gathering her belongings. On impulse, she scratched out a note for the inn's owner.

Dear Mr. Tyler,

Thank you so much for allowing me to work from your lovely home. It was such a peaceful day, and I accomplished more than I'd hoped. I so appreciate your generosity; and if you're certain it's not too much of an inconvenience, I'll plan to come back tomorrow.

Madeleine Houser

P.S. Your cat was a wonderful companion. He kept my feet toasty warm while I worked. What is his name? He is a "he," isn't he?

~~~

The following morning, Maddie gave instructions to the plumber and the electrician, who arrived on her doorstep at eight o'clock sharp. She hauled her laptop and reference books out to her little Mazda and drove the eight blocks to the nursing home to check in on her mother before heading out to the inn.

Mildred Houser had already been fed and dressed and was sitting in a chair in her room, staring out the window
~~~

with that vacant look Maddie had come to despise. It struck Maddie that her sixty-three-year-old mother looked older and far more frail than Ginny Ross did at eighty-four.

She took her mother's thin hand in hers. "Good morning, Mom."

No response.

"Your hands are cold. Do you want your sweater?"

Without looking at Maddie, her mother slowly stretched out her arm and, with birdlike motions, brushed at something invisible on the windowsill.

"It's a beautiful September day, Mom. Maybe we can go for a walk when I come this evening."

She might as well have been talking to the wall. Maddie sighed, went to the closet, and picked out a lightweight sweater. As she started to close the sliding door, she noticed something leaning in a far corner of the closet—the old canes she and Kate had bought for their mother when Mom had first started losing her balance. On impulse, Maddie chose one of the canes and tested it. It did ease the pressure on her ankle. Maybe she'd borrow it for a couple days. Mom rarely left her room anymore or even moved from her chair once the nursing staff got her out of bed.

She closed the closet door and went to drape the sweater over her mother's shoulders. "There," she said, patting the frail hand. "I can't stay long this morning, but I'll check in on you before dinner tonight."

Her mother turned slowly from the window and looked from the cane to Maddie's face. For one brief moment, Maddie thought she saw a spark of recognition in the rheumy eyes. But as quickly as it had come, it was gone, and Maddie was left with a familiar dull ache in her heart. *Oh, Mom. I miss you so much.*

~~~

Maddie arrived at the inn before nine o'clock. She hadn't noticed before what a beautiful setting the charming house occupied. With a shelterbelt of Osage orange trees to the east and a stand of cottonwoods far to the south, the house stood sentinel on the Kansas plains. A late September cool spell had left the trees and shrubs tinged with a hint of the autumn to come, but the pink- and peach-colored roses climbing the trellis by the front porch were still in bloom.

Maddie got out of her car and breathed in the fresh country air. She slung her computer bag and purse over one shoulder and tucked the sack lunch she'd brought under her arm. Attempting to use her mother's cane properly, she climbed the steps to the wide, wraparound porch. She found the key in the mailbox beside the front door, just where Ginny had said it would be. Letting herself in, she went down the hallway to the dining room to set up her laptop. On the table, she discovered a message penned in a tidy masculine script on the back of the note she'd written the day before.
~~~

Dear Ms. Houser,

I'm delighted that you enjoyed the time you spent here yesterday. I apologize for the dust and cobwebs. The inn has been a bit neglected since my wife's death. But I'm glad you were able to make use of it. Please do continue to come for as long as you like.

And thank you for washing up the dishes. I'm sorry to have left the kitchen in such a mess. I rarely have guests at the inn during the week, but I did have someone drop in Tuesday night and didn't get a chance to clean up before I left to teach my eight o'clock class. I shall try to do better in the future.

Arthur Tyler

P.S. The cat's name is Alex. And yes, "he" is a he. I hope he hasn't been a pest. As you probably discovered, he has no claws so is banned from the great outdoors, but please feel free to shoo him downstairs if he becomes a problem. Ginny tells me that you have a horrendous deadline, and I'd hate to be responsible—even by proxy—for you not meeting it. (And I confess that I haven't read any of your writing yet, but if Ginny has her way, that shall be remedied very quickly.)

Arthur Tyler

(I felt I needed to sign this once again, since I waxed so eloquent after my original signature.)

What a charming old gentleman Ginny's friend was! Maddie smiled as she tucked the note into her computer bag. Ginny had said Arthur Tyler was retired but still taught English at one of the colleges in Wichita. She wondered if his lengthy missive was due to the English professor in him or merely to loneliness. A little of both, she suspected.

She finished setting up her laptop and started a pot of coffee. While it brewed, she tidied up the kitchen. She found a dust cloth and a can of spray furniture polish under the sink and took them out to the dining room, where she polished the tables and buffet. She hated dusting her own house, but it was different cleaning someone else's. Besides, it was the least she could do if the proprietor wouldn't let her pay him for the time she was spending in his bed-and-breakfast.

When the luscious aroma of Irish cream café reached her nostrils, Maddie filled a large mug and set it beside her laptop. But before she opened the computer file that contained her novel, she penned another note to Mr. Tyler.

Dear Mr. Tyler,

Alex is not a pest at all! I've thoroughly enjoyed his company. I had a cat once myself, when I was a little girl. But since I began writing, I haven't had time to take care of one.

Please don't think another minute about the "dust and cobwebs." I didn't even notice.

Maddie read the last line again. It wasn't exactly the truth. She scratched out a word and changed the sentence to read: *I barely even noticed.* She smiled to herself, signed the note, then put her fingers on her laptop's keyboard and delved happily into Anne Caraway's world.

three

Arthur Tyler pulled into the driveway with a weary sigh. The weathered sign in front of the house said, "Welcome to Annabeth's Inn," but it would never again feel like a welcoming place to him. Not without Annabeth—his Annie.

If this was what thirty-nine felt like, Art couldn't imagine living to be as old as his friend Ginny. Ginny Ross had been Annie's friend first, but as the cancer had sucked away Annabeth's young life, the older woman had taken Art under her wing. As if she and Annie were coconspirators, Ginny's friendship had gradually been transferred to him. It was Annie's last gift to him, and he was grateful. Sometimes Ginny was the only one who could cheer him up when the loneliness and confusion threatened to overwhelm him.

Annie had been gone for more than two years now. Sometimes it seemed like forever, and Art struggled to remember how the music of her voice had sounded, how her skin had felt beneath his touch. Other times, it seemed as though she would come bounding up the stairs any minute, wearing her pixie smile and that shimmer in her eyes that spoke of how much she loved him. He wasn't sure which scenario was worse.

He parked outside the garage, which was too full of Annie's garage-sale finds to make room for a vehicle. He'd fussed at her about that before she got sick. How he wished he could take back his cranky words, all the petty annoyances he'd ever griped about. He'd wasted so much time on things that didn't matter. Now, nothing mattered.

He slammed the door of his pickup and walked back down the drive to the mailbox. The first day of October had blown in on a chill wind, and he turned up the collar of his overcoat. He pulled down the arched door of the mailbox. Junk. A couple Christmas catalogs, a flier advertising Clayton's Oktoberfest celebration, and the gas bill, which would be outrageously high—even higher next month, now that he was leaving the heat on during the day for Ginny's writer friend. But what did he care? He had nothing else to spend his money on.

"Be still and know that I am God." The words floated through his brain, scolding him for his attitude. "Sorry, Lord," he whispered, as his footsteps crunched on the gravel drive. He walked around the house and turned the key in the side door that led to his basement apartment. He stepped into the empty foyer. A *thump, thump, thump* on the steps brought a slight smile to his face. Alex. Another gift from Annie. He'd hated cats—or thought he did—until

Annie had coaxed this mangy, stray alley cat off the highway and into his heart. Now Alex greeted him with a comical cross between a purr and a meow, arched his back, and rubbed up tight against Art's pant leg. Art stooped to scratch the soft chin. The vibrations of the feline "motor" *put-putted* against his hand.

"Hey, Alex. What's for supper?" He put the mail on the eating bar in the kitchenette and hung up his coat in the bedroom closet. Alex galloped after Art as he climbed the stairs to the inn to make sure Ginny's friend had locked the door behind her and hadn't left the coffeemaker on. He was happy that the woman was able to use the house as a getaway. It would have made Annie happy to think of having a real author staying in the house—writing in the house. Annie had read all of Madeleine Houser's books. Ginny had seen to that, giving her the most recent one each year for Christmas.

He'd never paid much attention to them. He leaned toward the classics and had read and reread Tolstoy, Dostoyevsky, Dickens, and even Jane Austen. They were what he taught at the university and were his passion. He'd always teased Annie about the fluffy romance novels she read. He assumed that was what Madeleine Houser wrote, though it was beyond him how someone Ginny's age could even remember what romance was. A wry smile touched his lips as he wondered if *he* remembered what it was.

Recalling that still, small voice that had reproved him earlier, Art brushed away the cynical thoughts.

As he came up the steps to the inn's dining room, his gaze landed on something under the table. He went to investigate and found a smooth wooden cane with an ornately carved handle. Apparently the author had dropped it and forgotten about it. Or perhaps she had been unable to reach it when it slipped beneath the table. He glanced around the room and noticed that the top of the buffet and the side tables gleamed in the afternoon sun. Madeleine Houser's dust rag had struck again. The woman had come to the inn to write for four days in a row now, and it seemed that each day he came home to a house looking tidier than it had the day before.

On the table, he spied a sheet of stationery filled with handwriting that was now familiar. They had gotten in the habit of writing little notes back and forth concerning the details of their arrangement. Art had rather enjoyed their brief correspondence. Perhaps the fact that he received such pleasure from an exchange of notes with an old woman he'd never set eyes on proved how desperately he needed to get a life.

He picked up the note and read.

Dear Mr. Tyler,

Once again, thank you for opening your home to me. The plumber finally got the water problems solved, but the electrical work is taking longer than expected, and the man who was to lay the flooring called this morning to say that he's a week behind schedule with his other jobs. I'm sorry. I certainly don't mean to burden you with my problems. I only mention them to explain why I continue to take advantage of your kind offer. Please, I want to say again, if this becomes a problem for you, I hope you'll say something. I could go to the library or somewhere else to write if this is not working out for you.

Also, I don't mean to pry, but I noticed that Alex seemed to be a bit listless this morning. I wondered if you'd noticed? Then this afternoon he disappeared. I hope he's okay. I've grown quite fond of my little foot-warmer.

Thank you again,
Madeleine Houser

Arthur set the note down and stooped to pick up Alex. "Are you feeling okay, Buddy?" The cat looked perfectly healthy, purring away in his arms. Art gave the furry chin a good scratching. "Maybe Ms. Houser just doesn't realize how old you're getting to be."

He wasn't sure if cat years were anything like dog years, but at least ten years must have passed since Annie had rescued Alex from the highway. Though the cat had been skinny as a snake, he had been full grown, so who knew how old he really was. The thought made Art feel old himself. And sad. He didn't need more loss in his life.

He put Alex on the floor and sat down at the table to reply to Madeleine Houser's note. Turning over her stationery, he wrote on the back:

Dear Ms. Houser,

First of all, please do not apologize again. I am delighted to have you here, especially as it seems that every evening when I come home, one less dirty dish sits in the sink and one more piece of furniture is cleared of dust. Housekeeping services were certainly not part of the agreement we made, but I must say I don't want to complain too loudly. In all seriousness, I appreciate the tidying up you've done more than you can know.

Second, please call me Art. I hear Mr. Tyler a hundred times a day from my students, and though you and I have never met, I'd like to think we could be on a first-name basis by now.

Third matter of business: As you've probably discovered, you left your cane here today. I found it under the table. I've left it leaning in the corner by the kitchen. Hope you didn't miss it too much.

And finally: As for Alex, I'll keep an eye on him, but I haven't noticed anything out of the ordinary. He's a bit of a couch potato, and like the rest of us, I suppose, he is getting along in years. But thank you for your concern. I'll tell him you asked after him.

He smiled to himself at his little joke, scrawled a happy face beside it, and signed his name. He hoped the old woman was getting as much enjoyment from their note swapping as he was. His step a bit lighter, he went down to his apartment to fix a sandwich and grade the essays his advanced English students had turned in.

four

By the end of the following week, Maddie had settled into a comfortable routine. She consulted with the workmen before leaving the house to run the day's errands and make a quick visit to the nursing home. She usually reached her makeshift desk in the inn's dining room by nine A.M.

On Friday morning, the electrician knocked on the back door at eight o'clock, and Maddie let him in as she headed out, loaded down with packages to mail. Miracle of miracles, she had the first half of the manuscript ready to ship off to Peggy Barton, the woman who proofread for her. Kate had called and asked her to get some things out of storage, so Maddie had those ready to mail as well.

When she'd talked to Kate Wednesday night, her sister had sounded as happy as a ladybug in a sunflower patch. Jed loved his job, and they loved their new neighborhood—and their all-in-one-piece home. Maddie felt a twinge of irritation that she'd been left to clean up after Kate and Jed. Though she hadn't spent much time at the house on Harper Street lately, if anything, it seemed things were in more disarray than ever when she came home each evening. She hoped it was simply an illustration of the adage that sometimes things had to get worse before they could get better.

"Call me if you need me, Joe," she shouted to the owner of Mason Electric as she closed the door on the mess with a heavy sigh.

At the post office, she got out of the car and went around to the passenger side, where she'd stacked the packages. Her ankle was much better. Though she still favored her left leg a bit, she'd returned her mother's cane when she'd gone to visit last night. Piling the parcels in her arms, she gave the car door a shove with one hip and started up the sidewalk that led to the post office.

As she approached the double doors, a dark-haired man came out. He held the door open for her.

"Thanks so much," she said, smiling at him over the tower of packages.

"No problem," he said. The smile he flashed in return did funny things to her insides.

Forget it, Houser, she admonished, catching the man's departing reflection in the glass. *He's probably married. Besides, you've given up on men, remember?*

The man stopped on the sidewalk to talk to an older gentleman who'd just stepped out of a maroon Monte Carlo. "Hey, Art. How's it going?" the older man said. "I was just telling Nellie that we never see you anymore. How's life treating you?" The door swung shut and Maddie missed the younger man's reply. Ah, small town life. Clayton was one of the last towns in America without home delivery, so the post office was a social hub. She liked the fact that everyone seemed to know everybody else here in this little burg. In her New York neighborhood, even on the rare occasion when she'd run into the same person twice, no one ever bothered to get a name or exchange more than polite nods.

She dropped off her packages, picked up her mail, and drove out to Annabeth's Inn. After two weeks of writing there each day, pulling into the inn's driveway had started to feel like coming home. Maddie wasn't sure if she would be able to write in the house on Harper Street once it was livable again. She was beginning to wish she hadn't prayed so hard for the plumber and electrician to hurry up. But of course, once the remodeling was done on Kate and Jed's house, Realtors and potential buyers would be interrupting her peace—unless she decided to buy the place herself.

She sighed and carried her things into the house, then set up her laptop on the dining room table. She had a set routine and quickly had the coffeepot going, a dust rag flying, and Mozart providing background music for it all. The smell of fresh coffee wafted into the front parlor where Maddie was cleaning; and she put away the dust rag, filled a large mug, and set to work on her novel.

When the clock chimed eleven thirty, Maddie could

hardly believe it. She had two thousand words to show for her diligence—along with a stiff spine. She pressed the keys, saving the file to her computer, then pushed her chair back and stood to stretch. Her gaze traveled down the hallway to the ornate staircase that led to the upstairs guest rooms. She'd been dying to explore the rest of the house but had been afraid to try the stairs on her sprained ankle. Gingerly she rotated her foot a few times and bent to rub it. The swelling was almost gone, the pain barely noticeable anymore. She'd dusted the entire first floor twice over the course of two weeks. Maybe it was time to see what kind of shape the second floor was in.

Thickly carpeted steps creaked under her weight, and she felt unaccountably guilty. But Ginny had told her that Mr. Tyler had said she was free to use any room in the house, so surely he wouldn't mind if she took a look around.

She was halfway up the stairs when the doorbell broke the silence and set Maddie's heart pounding. She crept back down the steps and peeked through the curtain covering the windowed front door. Ginny Ross's Volkswagen sat in the driveway, and Ginny herself stood on the porch.

Maddie opened the door, feeling herself flush like a child caught snooping under the Christmas tree. "Hi, Ginny." She laughed and put a hand to her heart. "You scared me. I was just about to take a tour of the upstairs."

Ginny held out a brown bag that bore the golden

arches of McDonald's. "I hope you haven't had lunch yet. I brought cheeseburgers."

"Bless your heart! Let's go eat. I hadn't thought about it until now, but I'm starved."

"Well, I can't stay too long. You have work to do, and I have a piano student coming early."

Maddie led the way to the dining room. She swept her books and papers to one side while Ginny opened the paper sack and took out two fat, wrapped burgers and a cardboard container overflowing with fries. The savory scent filled Maddie's nostrils and made her stomach growl in protest. She went to the kitchen for paper napkins and glasses of ice water, gratefully tossing the dry peanut butter sandwich she'd brought into the trash can under the sink.

Maddie joined Ginny at the table, and the older woman bowed her head and blessed their food, ending with, "And please be with Madeleine as she works on this project You have given her to complete. Help her to make that deadline."

"Thank you, Ginny," Maddie said, deeply touched.

"So how *is* the book coming along?" Ginny asked.

"Very well, I think. It's sometimes hard for me to tell. I get too close to my work to be objective. But I do know that if it weren't for this wonderful writing retreat you found for me, I'd still be limping along."

Ginny nodded approvingly. "Speaking of limping, your ankle seems to be better."

"Much, thank you."

"And the house? Are they making progress?"

"Slow but sure," Maddie said over a mouthful of cheeseburger. She swallowed and wiped a spot of ketchup from the corner of her mouth. "To tell you the truth, Ginny, I'm almost dreading the day they finish."

"Why ever would you say that?"

"Because then I won't have an excuse to come to this lovely place anymore. There seems to be something. . .special about this house." She sobered. "But I know I'm imposing on Mr. Tyler. I don't want to overstay my welcome."

"Nonsense," Ginny said. "You're as welcome here as you can be. Why, just the other day Arthur was telling me how you've been dusting and sweeping. I think he's the one who's beginning to feel guilty."

"It's nothing really. I just brush away a few cobwebs each morning while I'm waiting for the coffee to brew."

"The way Arthur talks, it's a lot more than that. By the way, Arthur is expecting guests at the inn this weekend, but he wanted me to tell you that the calendar is empty next week and you are welcome to come back then—and for as many weeks after that as you need."

"How nice. Mr. Tyler sounds like the sweetest man. I wish I could meet him sometime. I'd like to thank him in person."

A strange twinkle came to Ginny's eyes. "Well, maybe we can just arrange that one of these days."

As she watched her neighbor, it struck Maddie that

perhaps there was more than mere friendship between Ginny Ross and Arthur Tyler. How delightful to think of the lively Ginny having a romance. She'd never given the love lives of octogenarians much thought, but knowing Ginny the way she'd come to, suddenly she could picture it quite clearly. And if Ginny—at eighty-something—could find love again, maybe there was hope for Madeleine Houser somewhere down the road.

She pushed the thought away as quickly as it had come, chiding herself inwardly. She had made a decision five years ago, after Rob Clevenger broke her heart. Unfortunately Rob hadn't been the first. It seemed that marriage simply wasn't something God intended for her. She'd been blessed in many ways—with the warm relationship she had with her sister and her two nieces. With a successful career as a writer, and opportunities to travel all over the world. No, she should be satisfied and fulfilled with those things. Besides, she had Mom to take care of now. She didn't have time for romance.

"Don't you think so, Madeleine?" Ginny's voice interrupted her thoughts.

She had the decency to blush. "I'm sorry, Ginny. My mind drifted. What was that?"

Her neighbor leaned back and studied her for a moment. "I was just wondering if Arthur wouldn't be better off selling this house—the inn."

"I suppose it is an awful lot of work to keep the place up."

"Oh, it's not that. It's Annabeth. The memories must be thick here. They lived here their entire marriage, you know."

"Really? I didn't know that."

"Well, I, for one, think it's time he moved on. The man has a lot of good years left, and he's wasting them pining away for that woman. She was a dear woman—I'm certainly not denying that. But she's gone, and he needs to accept it."

Maddie smiled to herself. She wondered if Ginny realized how transparent she was being.

After Ginny left, Maddie pondered the things the older woman had said, and an idea began to take root. Perhaps if Maddie met Arthur Tyler—got to know him a bit—she could spur things along between him and Ginny Ross. If Mr. Tyler was as obtuse in the ways of romance as the men she'd known, he probably didn't have a clue that Ginny had feelings for him. Maybe there was the seed of a new novel in this. Her mind whirled with lovely possibilities that wove in and out of Anne Caraway's tale.

She scarcely looked up from her computer until the distant buzz of a lawn mower broke her concentration. She pushed back her chair and went to look out the parlor window. A husky, spike-haired teen in a baggy sweatshirt pushed a lawn mower back and forth across the front lawn. Maddie remembered Mr. Tyler mentioning in one of his notes that a high school student would be working in the yard on Fridays.

She went back to her keyboard and wrote steadily until the clock chimed four. Then she packed up her things and wrote a little note to Mr. Tyler. She still wasn't quite comfortable calling the old gentleman Art, as he'd requested. She opted for *Arthur* instead.

Dear Arthur,

My thank-yous surely fall on deaf ears by now.

She hoped the man wasn't hard of hearing. She certainly hadn't meant that literally. Ah, well, he was an English professor. Surely he could decipher her intent.

But I simply cannot leave this wonderful house each day until I've properly thanked my unseen host.

Once again, I had a most productive day writing. Sometimes the peace and quiet here are so perfect that I almost forget to take a break for lunch. Fortunately our dear, mutual friend remedied that today. Ginny Ross brought lunch out to the inn, and we had a wonderful visit. It made me realize that I've been at my house so seldom over the past few days, I've missed the pleasure of having Ginny for a neighbor. I'm not sure I've ever met such a sweet, selfless woman—and so energetic! She runs circles around me.

Maddie reread her note. She hoped her endorsement of Ginny wasn't too obvious. But then could one ever *be* too obvious with men? Giving a wry smile, she picked up the pen again.

Ginny says that you've given permission for me to come back next week. If you're certain that's not an imposition, I will happily take you up on the offer. The workers have made some progress on my house, but it's all going much slower than I imagined it could. At any rate, with the solitude I've found here at your inn, I'm finally beginning to believe I might make my deadline on this book after all. Thank you again, kind sir.

Have a nice weekend,
Madeleine Houser

On the way home, Maddie stopped by the post office to collect her mail. She'd had the mail from her New York apartment forwarded to Kansas, but it seemed slow in coming. Her mailbox had been depressingly empty all week. She bent and peered in the little windowed door. Ah, something was there. She dug in her purse for the key. Her box yielded a bill from Mason Electric and a postcard saying she had mail too large for the box.

She took the card to the counter and handed it to the clerk. The man went back into the bowels of the building and returned a minute later with a manuscript-sized envelope. What was this? Surely Peggy hadn't finished proofreading already. She took the package out to the car and attempted to tear open the Tyvek envelope. It wasn't budging, so she sliced it open with a nail file from her glove compartment.

Inside was the portion of her manuscript she'd sent to Peggy, ominously absent of red ink. A brief note lay on top under the wide rubber band that held the pages together:

> *So sorry to return this, Madeleine, but I've taken a full-time job and will no longer be able to proofread for you. I tried to contact you before you mailed the manuscript, but I never got an answer at the number you gave me and my E-mails aren't going through to you. I do hope this doesn't cause a problem.*

The implications of Peggy's note registered, and Maddie smacked the steering wheel with the flat of her hand. If it wasn't electricity and water leaks, it was proofreaders quitting. It truly would be a miracle if she turned this book in on time. She tossed the manuscript onto the pile of books and magazines in the passenger seat and put the key in the ignition. She really needed to go see her mother before she went home, but she wasn't sure she could handle one more depressing thing.

Tears came suddenly, and she wiped at them with the back of her hand. "Lord, I don't mean to be such a crybaby, but I don't think I can take much more. Please just help me to—"

A tapping sound on her car window broke through her prayer. She gave a little gasp, grabbed a tissue from the box on the floor in front of the passenger seat, and bent her head to dab discreetly at her damp cheeks before turning to see who had observed her little outburst.

She didn't know the man bent beside her car, wearing an expression of deep concern. Wait. No, it was the handsome man she'd seen in the post office the other day. She rolled the window down a few inches, curiosity drying her tears like a sponge.

"I'm sorry to bother you," the man said with an apologetic smile. "But. . .well, I couldn't help but notice you were upset. Is everything okay?"

Embarrassed as she was to have been caught crying, she was touched by the thoughtful gesture of this stranger—and a good-looking stranger at that. Such gorgeous blue eyes. "I–I'm okay," she told him, forcing a smile. "I just got some bad news in the mail."

"Oh? I'm sorry. I hope it's nothing too serious. . . ."

"Oh, no." She shook her head and affected a chuckle. "It's one of those things I'll probably laugh about in a few weeks, but right now it was just. . .too much. Thank you for asking, though. That was very thoughtful of you." She reached for the keys in the ignition, anxious to escape the man's sweet scrutiny.

He shrugged and ducked his head. "Sorry to have bothered you. I hope. . .I hope everything turns out okay."

"Don't worry. I'm sure it will."

He held up a hand in farewell and hurried across the street. In her rearview mirror, she watched him climb into an old Chevy pickup. She shook her head in wonder at the friendliness of these Midwesterners. No wonder Kate and Jed had loved raising their girls here in Clayton.

Feeling energized, Maddie drove to the nursing home and sat with her mother in the dining room while the older woman picked at the bland food they served her. Mom was quiet, but the vacant stare in her eyes seemed less pronounced, and she even flashed Maddie a conspiratorial look of disgust when Mr. Bender slopped his coffee on the white linen tablecloth. Maddie headed for home feeling hopeful again.

When she unlocked the kitchen door and flipped on the light, she was delighted to see the cupboard doors back on their hinges and the floor cleaned off in preparation for laying new tile.

"Thank You, Lord." Maddie's whispered prayer echoed hollowly in the empty room.

As she walked through the house that night, turning off lights and locking doors, she stopped in the living room in front of the old upright piano her nieces had practiced on. She leaned over the keyboard and played a tentative chord. The piano was rather rickety and sadly out of tune, but she scooted the bench out and sat down. Her rusty fingers explored the keys and soon found a simple little melody she'd learned as a child. She hadn't brought her piano or any of her music with her from New York—not that she read music well anyway. She mostly played by ear. Now she plinked out the song, enjoying the mindless activity. The piano had always been good therapy for her.

Maddie played for half an hour, then went to get ready for bed. As she washed her face and brushed her teeth, her mind replayed the day. She smiled to herself, thinking of her neighbor's crush on Arthur Tyler, and she drifted to sleep that night scheming of ways to get Ginny Ross and the innkeeper together.

But the tanned, handsome face of the kind stranger at the post office kept intruding on her dreams.

five

Arthur Tyler eased off the ramp and into the flow of traffic on I-135. It would be good to get home. He kept saying he was going to retire from this teaching job. The commute was getting old, and with winter coming, it would be worse. But if he did retire, what in the world would he do with his time? He could always start advertising the inn and get it running back at full capacity, but he hadn't had the heart for it since Annie. Still, it would beat driving an hour each way to work every day. He actually enjoyed the maintenance and odd jobs of keeping the inn up—even rather liked cooking simple breakfasts for weekend guests. It was the little touches he'd never been good with. Arranging fresh flowers, scented candles, and clean, colorful linens in each room had always been Annie's department.

Ms. Houser had inadvertently made it clear to him that he had no clue what it took to keep up with the simple housekeeping of the place. He'd been amazed to see the difference it made simply to have the cobwebs swept away and the tabletops polished. If he had enough paying guests, he could hire someone to do those things or perhaps even find a permanent boarder to do the housekeeping. But that would cut the significant income that one guest room could generate. Not that money was really an issue. Even after setting college funds aside for Annie's nieces, the inheritance she'd received when her parents died had made it possible for him to retire whenever he wanted. That was the trouble, though. He wasn't sure what he wanted.

Life had lost its sunshine, its certainty, when Annie left his world. It had been a long time since he'd felt passionate about anything. His friend Dave Sanders had suggested more than once that perhaps a change of place would provide the impetus he needed to jump-start his life. Maybe he did need to sell the inn and move away. But it was hard to imagine how leaving Clayton—and his church, and the people he and Annie had come to love—could make his life more fulfilling.

Madeleine Houser came to his mind. According to Ginny, the author had left her home in New York and moved to Kansas to be near her mother. If Art thought it would be difficult at his age, what must it be like for someone as. . .well, as settled as Ms. Houser must have been? Maybe he'd ask her about it. Their correspondence had deepened over the weeks she'd been coming to the inn to write, and the notes provided a bright spot in his otherwise mundane days.

He pulled in at a fast-food restaurant on the edge of town and grabbed a burger and fries before going home. Alex met him at the door, pawing at his legs, begging for a bit of hamburger. While Art and Alex shared supper, he tried to explain his dilemma in a note to the author.

Dear Ms. Houser,

I have been contemplating something, and it struck me today that you might provide some insight on the topic.

Quite frankly, I have felt rather "stuck" since the death of my wife. Though I can hardly picture it, friends have suggested that it might be wise to sell the inn and move away from Clayton and all the memories it holds for me. Since you've just made the kind of move my friends are advising, I wonder how you feel about their suggestion. I don't want to burden you with the task of giving a floundering soul advice, but if you have any quick thoughts on the subject, I'd certainly be more than grateful for the input.

I trust the writing is still going well. Again, I deeply appreciate all the housekeeping you've done. The inn is wearing a much brighter face these days. And if there is anything I can do to make your stay here more comfortable or conducive to meeting that deadline, by all means, please let me know.

Happy writing,
Arthur Tyler

He capped his pen and reread the note. He had to smile at the formal tone he affected whenever he wrote to Madeleine Houser. Quite different than the terse, hip notes he scribbled on his students' essays. Perhaps it was only natural for one to pander to the sensibilities of the audience one was addressing, but reading this brief note, he was reminded of the long letters he'd written his grandmother Tyler after he'd gone off to college. He'd often asked Grandmother's advice—sometimes when he'd already made up his mind about something—like marrying Annie. But it had been nice to have Grandmother confirm his decisions. On the rare occasion when Opal Tyler had offered a dissenting opinion, Art had always given it careful consideration.

His heart swelled at the memory. He left the note lying on the table in the dining room where Ms. Houser would find it in the morning. It might be nice to meet Ginny's friend someday. Tell her how much Annie had enjoyed her books. Maybe he should read one of the woman's novels himself. According to Ginny, Madeleine Houser was quite well known in her genre. There might be a marketing angle to it if he ever decided to advertise the inn again—provided, of course, that Ms. Houser didn't mind him dropping her name in his brochures. He doubted she would, though. Didn't most authors crave any publicity they could get?

~~~
~~~

Maddie read the note again, already composing a reply in her mind. She thought it rather odd that Mr. Tyler would ask advice of her, but she was glad for an opportunity to offer the inn's owner her opinion. Rubbing her chin thoughtfully, she picked up her pen.

Dear Arthur,

First of all, if we're going to be on a first-name basis, it must be mutual! Please call me Madeleine.

I admit I feel a bit strange trying to offer you advice. Surely you are much wiser and more qualified than I to make such a decision. But I suppose I do have my own experience to share (and I'll try not to write a novel—ha!). Perhaps you'll find a nugget of help in hearing what I've gone through.

I was perfectly happy living in New York. But my sister's husband was transferred out of state, and my mother lives at the nursing home here in Clayton. My sister convinced me that I could write anywhere. . .well, you know that story! At any rate, I made the move somewhat against my will and with an attitude that was less than Christian. For a while, I let that attitude fester, and as you can imagine, things only got worse.

Once I finally started assuming that God had a hand in this whole thing, I began to recognize many good things about the move. It caused me to step out of a box that had become a little too comfortable. Most of all, I'm happy to be near my mother during her final years. Even though Mom is in the latter stages of Alzheimer's and doesn't know me anymore, it's been a blessing to spend time with her.

Well, enough about me. Since I don't know you or the reasons your friends are recommending this move, it's hard for me to give advice. I also don't know where you stand with the Lord (although knowing Ginny's deep respect for you, I trust that you have a close relationship with Him). But I will say that I believe if you seek Him about this matter, He will guide you to the right decision. It may not seem right at first. It may be difficult and lonely for awhile, as my adjustment has been. But I have lived long enough to know that God can take a noxious weed patch and turn it into a sweet-smelling rose garden.

Maddie started to sign off, tickled that she'd found a way to campaign for Ginny again. But suddenly an idea came to her. She wondered why she hadn't thought of this before. She picked up the pen.

Since you felt free enough to ask for my input, might I take the liberty of asking for yours? Last week I received the unfortunate news that I've lost my proofreader. I understand that you teach English, and I wonder if you might know of someone among your associates who would be willing to do that sort of work for me. I have a wonderful editor at my publishing house, but what I need is someone to give my manuscript a once-over, checking for simple typographical and grammatical errors, inconsistencies in the story line. . .that sort of thing. It could even be a conscientious college student. If you know of someone who'd be willing to take on the task on rather short notice, I would be most appreciative. I have a January deadline that is beginning to terrify me! (Of course, I would expect to pay the going rate for the service.)

I'll be thinking of you as you mull over the decision facing you. And thank you in advance for any help you can provide regarding a proofreader.

Your friend,
Madeleine Houser

Six

Art locked the door to his office at the university and walked out to his parking space. His cell phone lay on the dusty seat of the truck, displaying a message warning. Once on the highway, he listened to the message.

Dustin Brevits, the high school kid who took care of the inn's lawn, was already a week overdue with the mowing. Now he'd gotten himself an after-school detention and was backing out on the responsibility again. Art punched the keypad and lobbed the phone onto the passenger seat. He had guests scheduled at the inn for Friday and Saturday nights. The recent rains and balmy weather had the grass growing faster, and by the weekend it was going to look like a jungle.

Art sighed. He'd just have to mow it himself. Not that he really minded the job, but it got dark so early these days that he usually watched the sun set on the drive home. Maybe he could rearrange some office appointments and get home early enough on Friday afternoon to at least mow the main lawns. The flowers would have to go without their much-needed deadheading.

He could see why Ms. Houser had been so frustrated over her lost proofreader. Nothing was more irritating than people who were not dependable. The thought caused him to slap the ball of his hand to his forehead. He'd meant to post something on the job board in the English department about needing a proofreader. Talk about unreliable!

But wait a minute. He'd been wanting to read one of Ms. Houser's novels anyway. Why didn't *he* offer to proofread it? Judging by her neatly penned notes, he doubted there would be much to mark on one of her manuscripts. Not to mention that he was beginning to feel rather guilty about the amount of housekeeping the woman was doing for him. He'd walked through the house last night and rejoiced at how spotless it was. He wouldn't have to do a thing to the main floor before the guests arrived. He would, however, need to clean the third-floor guest room they'd reserved. Ms. Houser's cane undoubtedly had not allowed her to brave the steep stairway to the attic room.

With one hand on the steering wheel and one eye on the traffic, he rummaged in his briefcase for a notepad and pen, then jotted down some cryptic reminders to himself.

He pulled into the inn's driveway just as a beautiful Kansas sunset splashed across the western horizon. He parked the pickup, jumped out, and walked back to the mailbox, marveling at shades of pink and turquoise and tangerine that he'd never seen any artist reproduce successfully. As he walked back to the entrance to his basement apartment, the crunch of gravel beneath his feet echoed in the still, fall air. How could he ever leave this place? Dave was crazy.

He threw his briefcase and jacket on the cluttered table and went to check out the upstairs. Alex met him at the top of the steps with his comical half-purr, half-meow greeting. The dining room table was empty. Hmmm. In the two-and-a-half weeks she'd been coming, Ms. Houser had failed to leave a note only one other time. Art checked the kitchen. She'd been here, all right. The clean coffee carafe, a soup bowl, and a cup and saucer were neatly stacked in the dish drainer. He was surprised at how disappointed he felt at the absence of that note. Maybe Dave was right after all. Maybe he seriously needed to get a life.

Alex pattered after him as he climbed the carpeted stairs to the second floor and opened the door to the narrow stairwell that led to the attic suite the weekend guests had requested. This had been his and Annie's room before the inn had become so successful and they'd decided to finish the basement apartment and open the suite to guests. Art let his hand rest on the brass doorknob for a moment, steeling himself. It was still difficult to enter this space that held so many sweet, intimate memories.

He flipped the light switch and climbed the steps,

feeling the air grow chill as he reached the top. He walked over to the antique dresser on the far wall. Fine dust coated the smooth oak surface, and the beveled mirror that hung over the dresser was dim with grime. He ducked under the low-hanging eaves and stepped into the modern bathroom that adjoined the room. A bulb was out on the Hollywood strip lighting that surrounded the mirror. The window that looked out over fallow fields to the north of the house was open an inch, and Art noticed that the sill was littered with dead flies. A tiny spider scurried down the drain of the large whirlpool tub. Art made a mental note to bring up some cleaning supplies and bug spray after supper.

As he stepped back into the room and pulled the bathroom door shut behind him, his gaze fell on an oval frame, convex glass protecting the photograph inside. As much as he wanted to turn away, he was drawn to the picture like steel to a magnet. The sepia-toned image looked as authentic as the antique frame—just as Annie had intended. But the stoic couple standing side by side in the photograph was Art and Annie Tyler, circa 1993. It had been taken on their Colorado honeymoon at one of those Old West novelty portrait places in Durango. Annie had picked out their costumes, including the handlebar mustache Art sported in the portrait.

Art ran his fingers over the glass, gently wiping the dust from the image. A lump came to his throat as he gazed through the glass into Annie's eyes. Though her expression was stern and posed—as the long exposure time of the old tintype cameras necessitated—Annie's eyes held a distinct twinkle.

Art remembered the day as if it were yesterday. Once he had stepped from the dressing room wearing the Western duds and the dark mustache that matched his hair, Annie had dissolved in hysterical giggles. The photographer had a hard time capturing the serious pose Annie desired. But Annie had proudly framed the resulting print and penned the accompanying label, *Mr. and Mrs. Arthur Tyler,* in her flowing calligraphy.

"Come on, Alex," Art said, shaking his head to clear away the poignant memory. "We've got work to do."

Tail high, the cat followed him downstairs.

~~~

Maddie stared at the note, not quite sure how she should respond. Arthur Tyler had offered to proofread her manuscript. It would be wonderful to have an English professor read for her and especially helpful to get a male perspective on her story—even if that perspective did come from a generation or two before most of her readers were born. But how could she ask him for yet another favor? He had already offered her so much. Still, she was desperate.

Before she could change her mind, she picked up her pen and accepted his offer as graciously as she knew how.
~~~

Dear Arthur,

I sincerely hope you aren't making your offer to proofread my manuscript out of some altruistic, chivalrous sense of duty. Though we've never met, I "fear" that is just the kind of thing you would do. (Of course I use the word fear in a contrary sense. How I wish there were more men in my generation who possessed such a quality!)

I would love to take you up on your offer, under the following conditions:

1. *You allow me to pay you a fair wage for your work.*
2. *You are brutally honest in your critique of my writing. (You would do me no favors by being kind!)*
3. *You feel free to drop the job at any time, for any reason, without explanation or guilt.*

I will leave the first five chapters of my manuscript here, and if you are agreeable to these points, then have at it.

I know you must be weary of my gushing, but again, thank you so very much for all you've done to help me meet this deadline. You shall most definitely have a well-deserved mention in my acknowledgments page!

Have a lovely evening,
Madeleine Houser

That task out of the way, she plugged her computer in and set to work. She finished chapter twenty-seven but found herself at a loss as to what should come next.

Standing to stretch her cramped muscles, she walked from room to room on the main floor, failing to notice the now-familiar and dear features of the house as she mulled over her story. No great insights came. She had learned not to panic when this happened—though it was hard not to when she was so close to her deadline.

Maddie paced the hallway that ran the length of the house, her sneakers making an annoying squeak with each step. As she came to the staircase in the foyer, she remembered that she had never explored the second floor since the day Ginny had waylaid her with the enticement of cheeseburgers. Maddie's ankle had completely healed, and suddenly her novel was forgotten as she trotted up the stairs.

Three doors off the main hallway stood open, and Maddie walked first into a sitting room, part of a suite decorated in a Victorian motif, ruffled and elegant with a wonderful old porcelain claw-foot tub in the bathroom.

The room adjacent to the suite was more austere, with its Art Deco oak furniture and wall coverings. She meandered slowly through each room and back again, lingering over the trinkets thoughtfully arranged atop the antique dressers and armoires. The rooms were much as she had imagined, fitting the style of the old Victorian home, yet with modern comforts seamlessly woven in.

Obviously a great deal of loving care and no small measure of creative talent had gone into the decorating of these rooms. Annabeth Tyler had kept abreast of the world of interior design.

Maddie actually grew excited, thinking of a whole new part of the house she could dust and polish. She would earn her keep yet.

As she went back into the hallway to go downstairs, another door—this one closed—caught her eye. Expecting it to be locked, she tried the painted brass knob and was surprised when it swung outward, revealing a narrow, carpeted stairway. Feeling like a trespasser, she climbed the steps, relieved to discover that the room at the top was another cozy guest suite. Stooping to peer out the dormered window at the head of the stairway, she gave a little gasp at the beauty of the vista beyond. The window looked out over a Kansas patchwork of fields, and a row of ancient cottonwood trees stood against a backdrop of sky the color of sapphires.

Maddie knelt there for a long time, realizing again her surprise at how deeply this open sky and prairie landscape spoke to her spirit. The majesty of New York City paled by comparison.

Finally she stood and explored the suite, delighted to find a low bookcase filled with her favorite authors. Her eyes widened as she spotted hardcover copies of her first four novels lined up on the bottom shelf. Ginny had said that

Annabeth Tyler had been a fan. She wondered if these were Mrs. Tyler's copies. The book jackets were in pristine condition, as though the books had never been read, but then some people removed the jacket before they read a book.

She walked across the room, peeked into the bathroom, and took in the large, modern bath, complete with whirlpool tub. Mr. Tyler must be expecting guests for the weekend, for the room sparkled. Every chrome fixture shone to a mirror finish, and every wood surface glowed with a warm patina. The room still smelled of lemon oil and Pine-Sol. Maddie had begun to wonder if the inn ever had guests anymore, but here was her answer. Now she did feel as though she were trespassing, suddenly wanting to escape the room lest she leave it in less than pristine condition for the people who were obviously expected.

As she exited the bathroom, her gaze was drawn to an old portrait on the wall in front of her. A young couple posed staidly, side by side, staring straight ahead. Maddie had seen similar photographs while researching her historical novels. It always fascinated her to see such ordinary, often oddly familiar faces staring back from the past. This portrait was no exception. The convex glass that encased the photograph had the wavy quality typical of old glass, making it a bit difficult to see the portrait clearly, but the faces intrigued her—the glint of mischief so apparent in the woman's eyes. And the man reminded her of someone. She crossed her arms and rested her chin in one hand, trying to think of who it was.

Perhaps he was someone famous, someone she'd come across in her research once upon a time. Or maybe he just had one of those universally familiar faces.

Her fascination grew when she read the label at the bottom of the frame: *Mr. and Mrs. Arthur Tyler*. Judging by their formal clothing, this might have been their wedding portrait. What a handsome young man Arthur Tyler had been. She could almost picture what he must look like now—the black curls and mustache grown white, the smooth planes of his face tanned like leather and crinkled with laugh lines. She could hardly wait to meet the man in person and see if her conjectures were accurate. If they were, she could certainly understand Ginny's infatuation.

She glanced quickly around the room, hoping to discover a more recent portrait of the Tylers, but the only other frame in the suite held a faded, silvered mirror. Maddie studied her reflection for a moment, sweeping her hair up off her neck and twisting it into a wispish chignon like the one Annabeth Tyler wore in the portrait. Maddie had often thought she'd been born several generations too late. Glancing back at the portrait on the wall and the handsome figure the young Arthur Tyler cut, a strange ache of longing came over her.

All the heroes in her novels were men of centuries long past. Men of honor and integrity. Gentle men whose strength didn't depend on vulgarity and macho blustering. The only peers she'd ever met who had those qualities were spoken for.

She secretly feared that no one was left who had the traits she craved in a man. She let her hair fall limply to her shoulders and sighed.

As she descended the stairs, an idea sparked within her. She'd been looking for a face for Jonathan Barlowe, the character in her novel who would sweep her hapless heroine off her feet and into his heart. She had certainly found him. A smile pulled at the corners of her mouth. She wondered how Mr. Tyler would feel if she told him that his portrait had provided a model for one of her characters. An involuntary shiver crept up her spine at the thought. No. She couldn't make herself that vulnerable. Not when she had yet to meet the man. It must be her little secret for now. But she knew she would come up to this room each day to gaze into the eyes of her new hero before she went back, inspired, to her computer. Ah, how she envied Anne Caraway.

Seven

Art thanked the postal clerk, slipped the new book of stamps into his shirt pocket, and started through the post office door, stuffing his wallet into his back pocket as he walked. He glanced up in time to hold the door for an attractive young woman who was, like him, preoccupied, stuffing her gloves and keys into her purse. They almost collided, politely skirted around each other, then, in tandem, did a double take.

It was the woman from the white Mazda—the one he'd seen the week before crying over some bad news the mail had brought.

Recognition sparked in her green eyes, and she flashed a little smile. "Oh, hi there," she said, her cheeks flushing a lovely shade of peach.

He didn't want to embarrass her, but he took a risk, keeping his tone lighthearted. "You look considerably happier than the last time I saw you here."

The blush on her cheeks spread and deepened.

"Everything worked out fine," she said, looking up at him with a sheepish grin.

He started to say something then stopped and turned to watch as Mabel Bachman, the elderly wife of Clayton's mayor, shuffled toward them, weighed down with a bulky stack of packages. Art hurried to hold the door open for the elderly woman. Green Eyes gave a little wave and hurried on toward her car; and by the time Art had helped Mrs. Bachman with the door to the inner office, the Mazda was crawling down the street, headed north.

Art felt strangely disappointed. He'd meant to introduce himself to the attractive stranger. He didn't think she was married. No wedding ring. He'd noticed as she stuffed her gloves into her bag. Somehow he couldn't picture a married woman driving that sporty Mazda—especially not with a passenger seat that looked like it served as a filing cabinet and library rolled into one. Not that he planned to pursue this green-eyed beauty. She must be new to Clayton. He'd never seen her before, and he knew just about everyone in town by face, if not by name. He thought about asking around to see if any of his golf buddies knew who she was, but he could just hear the ribbing they'd give him if he mentioned a pretty young woman. As it was, his friends were constantly trying to set him up with somebody's cousin or stepsister or the former college roommate of a buddy's wife. No, thank you. He did not want to go there.

Art drove home, fed Alex, and fixed a bologna sandwich, which he took upstairs to eat while he read Madeleine Houser's note of the day. A sheaf of manuscript pages lay neatly on the dining room table. Good. The woman must have agreed to allow him to proofread her manuscript. He went into the kitchen for a glass and some ice cubes, bending to peer out the kitchen windows as he ran fresh tap water over the ice. Outside, the overgrown lawn rippled in the breeze. Art made a mental note to remember to come home early enough on Friday to get it mowed before the weekend guests arrived.

Back in the dining room, he read the note, smiling at the author's list of rules and her promise to list him in her acknowledgments for the book. He ran a hand through his hair. He might have to think of a graceful way to extricate himself from that dubious honor if the book turned out to be drivel. He would never hear the end of it from his colleagues at the university if his name appeared on the acknowledgments page of a schmaltzy romance novel.

Brushing bread crumbs from his hands, he pushed his sandwich plate away and drew the manuscript in front of him. He pulled a pen from his shirt pocket and uncapped it. Alex jumped into his lap and turned 360 degrees to brush his tail across Art's nose before finally settling in his lap.

"Hey, Buddy, what do you think? Am I going to like this lady's writing?" He stroked the cat's thick fur, and Alex revved his feline motor in response.

Running one hand absently down the length of the cat's back again and again, Arthur Tyler began to read.

~~~

Friday morning, Maddie went out to the garage, loaded down with her computer bag and the reference books she would need. Her mind on a new scene for Anne Caraway's story, she turned her keys in the ignition. Nothing.

Oh, great! She tried again with the same results. Sighing, she got out of the car and went around to open the hood. She knew as much about automobiles as she did about computers—almost nothing. There didn't seem to be any smoke, nor were any liquids dripping or spewing, so she slammed the hood down and ran inside to call a mechanic.

An hour later, with her Mazda at Bud's Automotive and driving a monstrous old Buick compliments of Bud, Maddie headed out.

She was already behind schedule, but she hadn't had the energy to see Mom the night before, so she stopped by the Clayton Market and picked up a bouquet of rather sad-looking daisies and carnations and drove to the nursing home. Mom was having another bad day, fidgeting and sputtering nonsensical syllables in a tired voice. She didn't seem to know Maddie was there.

Maddie stayed just long enough to transfer the flowers
~~~

to an unbreakable vase and to visit with the nurse about her mother's latest medical checkup. She felt guilty about not spending more time with Mom, but what difference did it make when her mother didn't know her from the nurse's aide who came to deliver her breakfast tray?

Maddie drove out to the inn, feeling discouraged and depressed. But as soon as the old Victorian house came into sight, her spirits lifted, as they did every time she pulled into the inn's driveway. She tried not to think about how close the workmen were to finishing the remodeling on Jed and Kate's house. When the last tile was in place, she would have no excuse to come out here anymore.

Shaking off the thought, she let herself in, set up her computer, and immediately climbed the two flights of stairs to visit her new hero. The man behind the oval glass was as handsome as she remembered—as handsome as he'd been in her dreams.

Again, she was struck by how familiar he seemed. That often happened with her characters. She would have a vague picture of a character in mind, only to open up a catalog or magazine and see the perfect face staring back at her. She always clipped pictures of her characters for inspiration. But Anne Caraway's hero had been a long time in making himself known. Maddie memorized the masculine contours of the young Arthur Tyler's face, the square jaw and the steel gaze of his pale eyes. Though she couldn't tell from the sepia-toned photograph, she imagined his eyes to be a mesmerizing shade of blue gray. Oh, to have been born a few decades earlier!

Maddie studied Annabeth Tyler's image—the playful glimmer in her eyes, the love on her face so tangible and compelling. Inspired, Maddie hurried downstairs to capture that passion on the computer screen.

She typed steadily, breaking for a quick cup of coffee and a bagel she'd bought that morning at Clayton's newly opened Main Street Deli. The story flowed, and finally Maddie could visualize the perfect ending. Her fingers flew across the keyboard, anxious to finish her tale so she could read it all over again and add in the subtle nuances of detail and characterization that imbued a story with Madeleine Houser's unique style.

Shortly after three o'clock, the sound of a motor revving outside startled her. Then she remembered that this was the day that high school kid mowed the inn's expansive lawn. Her concentration broken, she pushed back her chair and stood to stretch and knead the kinks from her spine.

She walked through the hallway into the front parlor and pushed the heavy curtains aside. Though he had his back to her, Maddie could see that the person pushing the mower wasn't the burly, spike-haired teen who usually came. This guy had shiny black hair that curled slightly at the nape of his tanned neck. And he was older—about her age, Maddie guessed. He was tall and slender, but even beneath the long-sleeved T-shirt he wore, she could see taut muscles flex as he maneuvered the push mower across the autumn-brittle grass.

As the man reached the edge of the driveway and turned the mower toward the house, Maddie took in a sharp breath and let the curtain fall back over the window. She knew that man. Heart thumping, she pulled the curtain aside and peered out again. It was the guy from the post office. The thoughtful man who'd caught her crying over Peggy's returned manuscript.

She tried not to acknowledge the disappointment she felt at discovering he apparently was employed doing odd jobs. Not only was it small-minded and judgmental of her, but she was jumping to conclusions. "Besides," she chided in a whisper, "you're not in the market for a man, Houser. Remember?"

She watched a little longer. But when she went back to the dining room and sat down at her computer, she'd lost her focus. She kept thinking about the handsome man from the post office. The man now outside, mowing the lawn. An odd sensation nudged the back of her mind—something she couldn't quite put her finger on. But it nagged at her.

Finally she heard the lawn mower's engine cut off and a few minutes later the sound of tires crunching on the gravel drive. She looked at the clock over the stairwell. It was time to leave anyway. She'd toyed with the idea of staying until Mr. Tyler came home some night. She could finally meet the man and perhaps put in a good word for Ginny. But tonight wasn't the time for that. Seeing the stranger from the post office here at the inn had left her feeling oddly disconcerted. She wanted nothing more than to go home and hibernate.

~~~

Art delivered the lawn mower to Mike and Milt's Sharpening Service and drove back to the inn. When he pulled into the drive, he saw that Madeleine Houser's old Buick was gone. The inn looked neat and tidy, sitting on the freshly cut lawn. Art admired his handiwork with satisfaction. If the weather cooperated, he could pick up the mower next week and park it in the garage, all sharpened and greased and ready to go for a new season. But if this Indian summer persisted, he'd probably have to cut the grass at least once more before winter set in.

He had to admit that he'd rather enjoyed the task of mowing. The sun on his face, an October breeze cooling his skin, and the physical exertion gave him a feeling of gratification and. . .was it hope? That seemed a little drastic; yet the more he thought about it, the more he realized that hope was exactly the emotion that welled within him.

The verse from Genesis 8 that Pastor Rennick had read last Sunday floated through his mind: "*While the earth remains, seedtime and harvest, and cold and heat, and summer*
~~~

and winter, and day and night shall not cease." Of course the verse referred to God's promise to Noah that He would never again destroy the earth by a great flood. Still, as Art looked north across the highway to the ripening milo fields and as he gazed at the trees in their dying autumn glory, he felt the hope of God's promise bloom in his heart. Tragic things happened. Yet in the midst of them, if one were watchful, one could see God's beauty manifested just as it was in the gold and scarlet and russet of the dying leaves. Life went on, and God gave one strength and courage to keep living. Only in Him was there the assurance of tomorrow, of springtime after a long winter, of a new harvest in the field.

Art slammed the door of the pickup and walked toward the side entrance of the old house. "Thank You, Father," he whispered over the lump that swelled his throat.

~~~

After dinner, Alex comfortably ensconced in his lap, Art sat in his recliner, Madeleine Houser's manuscript on his knee and a red pen at the ready. The cap mostly remained on the pen, however, for Art was captivated by the story. He had read two chapters the afternoon before and had immediately been impressed—and sheepishly contrite over his premature and hasty judgment of Ms. Houser's writing. Now well into the third chapter, he was amazed at the way the author's sensibilities seemed to be informed from his own
~~~

generation, in spite of the fact that the book was set in the nineteenth century. It was a rare author who could make him feel that the book had actually been penned in 1871, yet who spoke to the mind-set of a contemporary reader.

And the woman had obviously done her research. The historical details were sharply accurate. Her portrayal of the historic Chicago fire was chilling. He could almost hear the flames from the great conflagration cracking and snapping around him. Not only that, but her characterizations were multilayered with intricately woven relationships that kept him wanting to turn pages. He especially liked the hero. Not usually one for love stories, Arthur found himself intrigued by Jonathan Barlowe and could easily identify with this flawed man.

He stopped reading only long enough to scribble a note to Madeleine Houser, telling her to leave him every chapter she had ready without delay.

I am enthralled by your story, Ms. Houser. I had no idea what I've been missing all these years. I will finish these five meager chapters you've left me long before bedtime, and then I face the prospect of an entire weekend not knowing the fate of Anne Caraway, precocious little Charlie, and, of course, the quintessential hero, Jonathan Barlowe. (Please do not tell me you are one of those cruel writers who kill off beloved characters for no good reason.)

Art drew a happy face beside that last sentence, lest she take offense—or lest she *were* one of those cruel writers. He signed his brief note, picked up the manuscript again, and was soon transported to the Chicago of 1871.

eight

By Monday morning, Maddie had her Mazda back—complete with a new battery and spark plugs, plus a bill for almost two hundred dollars. But it ran like a top. She packed up her computer and books and left for her morning visit to the nursing home before going out to the inn. The tile layers had finally arrived, and she had to skirt around the beefy father-son team and their assorted toolboxes and equipment to reach the back door. She'd almost made her escape when the telephone rang.

After renegotiating the maze, she reached the phone. "Hello?"

"Could I speak to Madeleine Houser, please?" a deep voice asked.

"Yes, this is Madeleine."

A long silence came from the other end, and for a minute, Maddie thought she'd been cut off. "Hello?"

"Oh. . .yes. . .I'm sorry. This is Arthur Tyler. . .from Annabeth's Inn?"

"Oh, yes, Mr. Tyler. Hello there." The low, gravelly voice on the other end was just as Maddie had imagined Arthur Tyler would sound.

She heard the muffled sound of a hoarse cough. "I apologize," he said. "I seem to be coming down with something. I was wondering. . .were you planning on working out at the inn today?"

"Well, yes, I was. But I certainly don't have to. Would it be better if I didn't?"

"No. No. Please come ahead. I just wanted to let you know that I'm going to stay home in bed today. I didn't want you to be alarmed if you heard noises coming from the apartment below. I—"

"Maybe it would be best if I didn't come today. I don't want to disturb—"

"No. Please. I'm not trying to discourage you from coming at all. Judging by the way I feel right now, I'll probably sleep all day. I'll have no reason to set foot upstairs, and it won't bother me one bit to have someone in the inn. I'm used to having guests overhead. I just wanted to warn you that someone would be here."

The younger half of the tile-laying partnership pounded a rubber mallet noisily on the floorboards, and Maddie held her breath. She would get exactly nothing written today if she stayed home and tried to work in this zoo. "Well. . . If you're sure?"

"Very sure. Please, make yourself at home." Mr. Tyler

cleared his throat again and gave a gruff chuckle. "I might warn you, though, that I'm calling dibs on the famous foot-warming cat today."

Maddie laughed into the receiver. "I understand completely. It sounds like you need Alex's services worse than I do."

She put the phone back in its cradle and stared at it, unseeing. Because of the photograph in the attic bedroom, Maddie had a distinct image of Arthur Tyler—even if it was a half-century old. She felt she knew much of his personality through the delightful notes he left for her, but it was so strange to have a voice to put to those notes. He had almost become like one of her characters—an intangible, yet beloved presence in her life. But hearing his throaty voice had made him seem all too real, and suddenly she felt very odd about going out to the inn, knowing he would be in his apartment.

The clatter of a slamming toolbox lid brought her to her senses. She didn't have much choice but to go. Besides, Mr. Tyler was expecting her, and she didn't want to call him back and risk getting him out of bed. Climbing over the flooring materials that littered the kitchen floor, she grabbed her computer and briefcase and escaped out the back door.

On a whim, she stopped by the Main Street Deli and picked up two Styrofoam tubs of chicken noodle soup. She'd heat up one for lunch and leave the other in the refrigerator for Arthur Tyler's supper. That ought to be good for what ailed him, and it was another small way she could show her appreciation.

~~~

Arthur Tyler set his cell phone carefully on his bedside table, flipped off the lamp, and sat in bed, staring at the opposite wall. Odd. If he didn't know better, he would have guessed the voice of the woman he'd just spoken to belonged to someone younger. Much younger.

But with his sinuses so clogged he could scarcely hear, who knew how distorted his perception had been? He shook his head and reached for a tissue, then blew his nose so forcefully that Alex jumped up from his nest at the foot of the bed and hissed.

"It's okay, Buddy. Go back to sleep." Art reached out to stroke the gray-and-white fur that now stood comically on end.

The cat turned two full circles and plopped back down on the bed. Apparently reassured, Alex rested his head on his front paws and resumed purring. Art tucked his feet into the warm spot the cat provided, slid beneath the fluffy down comforter, and drifted off into a Nyquil-induced haze.

He awakened some time later to the sound of footsteps overhead. Alex jumped off the bed and trotted down the hallway to investigate. Art rolled over and glanced at the clock on the bedside table. It read 8:45. That would be
~~~

Madeleine Houser. His head throbbed. Stifling a cough, he shrank under the covers.

Art heard Alex pad softly up the stairs, then the sound of feminine cooing and clucking floated down. There went his foot-warmer. *Traitor.*

Curious, he crept out of bed and went to the foot of the stairs. He heard the refrigerator open and close, then the sound of water running and the coffeemaker beginning its cycle. With his stuffy nose he couldn't smell the brew, but he sure wouldn't have minded having a cup. The heat would feel great on his scratchy throat.

He was sorely tempted to throw a sweatshirt over his T-shirt and sweatpants and go up and introduce himself to the author. But he dare not expose her to whatever nasty bug he had. At her age, a virus like this could easily turn into pneumonia. With one ear to the sounds upstairs, he went to his kitchenette and boiled a mug of water in the microwave. He scooped a couple spoonfuls of stale instant coffee into the hot water. Wholly unsatisfying, but it would have to do. Someday he'd remember to buy a coffeemaker for his apartment.

Art heard Ms. Houser talking again upstairs, presumably to his faithless feline. He took his steaming mug and walked over to the partition separating the stairway from his living area, careful to stay out of sight in case the woman should be at the head of the stairwell. He didn't want to give her a heart attack.

"Come on, Kitty," he heard the youthful voice from the telephone say. "Go on. Get back down there. You need to stay with your master. Go on, Alex. I don't have anything for you today."

How sweet. She was trying to coax Alex back downstairs. He liked this lady. And her voice—there was just something about it that struck a chord with him. It had a musical quality with the faintest hint of the East Coast in her accent. He was having trouble making that voice match the picture of the author he had in his mind.

Feeling light-headed and groggy, Art went to his room and crawled back into bed. He drifted off to sleep, thinking how nice it was to have someone upstairs puttering around in the kitchen and making use of his poor, neglected home.

~~~

Maddie had a hard time concentrating, knowing that Arthur Tyler was practically right underneath her. Several times she heard his deep, wracking cough and was tempted to heat up the chicken soup she'd brought and take it down to him. But she didn't want to embarrass the man by catching him in his bathrobe—or worse.

She ignored Alex as she did some editing on the chapter she'd written the day before, and finally the cat sauntered back down the stairs. Maddie tried to write the first draft of a new scene, but her concentration was shot.
~~~

She thought about putting a CD into her computer, but she was afraid the music would bother her ailing host.

At noon, she heated up a container of the soup for lunch. Careful as she was to tread lightly, the floors in the old house creaked with every step. It was a wonder Mr. Tyler didn't storm up the stairs and order her to leave.

At two o'clock, having accomplished painfully little, she packed up her laptop and books. Before she left, she wrote a brief note to Arthur Tyler.

Dear Mr. Tyler,

I'm so sorry you're ill. I hope I didn't disturb you too much today. It was probably a bad idea for me to come here with you home sick. I'm afraid every creak and squeak in the house sounded like a herd of camels to you. I do apologize and hope you're feeling better by the time you read this. I've left you some of the new deli's wonderful chicken noodle soup. As you may know, studies show that chicken soup actually has medicinal value for cold sufferers. I hope you enjoy it. Even if it doesn't cure what ails you, it is delicious.

Perhaps it would be best if I don't come back to the inn until you let me know that you are well and able to return to work.

Praying for your speedy recovery,
Madeleine Houser

P.S. I apologize for "stealing" Alex away from you for awhile this morning. I hope you don't think I was enticing him with kitty treats or something. I promise you, he came of his own accord.

Maddie drew a smiley face after her postscript and, out of habit, jotted her initials at the end of the note.

Driving home, she fought discouragement at losing a whole day of writing. She simply must learn to discipline herself to work under adverse conditions.

Pulling into her drive a few minutes later, she saw Ginny Ross sweeping the first of autumn's offerings off her own front porch. She parked the car in the garage and went around to the front of the house to talk with her neighbor.

"Well, hello there, Miss Madeleine," Ginny called out as Maddie came up the walk. She wielded her broom to scoot a giant red maple leaf onto the grass.

"Hi, Ginny." Maddie eyed Ginny's broom, then looked up into the branches of the half-dozen oaks and maples in the yard that had yet to shed their autumn coats. "That's kind of a losing battle, don't you think?" she teased.

"Oh, I know it is, but it's good exercise. Besides, I enjoy being out-of-doors on a day like this."

"This is glorious weather, isn't it?"

"I'll say." Ginny leaned the broom against the porch

railing and put her hands on her hips. "So, how many words did you write today?"

Maddie sighed. "Not very many, I'm afraid. Mr. Tyler was home sick and I just couldn't concentrate."

A strange expression crossed Ginny's face. "Arthur was at home? Did you meet him?"

"Oh, no. Like I said, he was in bed sick, the poor man. He has a terrible cough."

Ginny clicked her tongue. "Oh, my. I don't suppose that was very conducive to a quiet day of writing."

"Oh, it's not that. It just felt strange to be in his house with him right downstairs."

Ginny didn't say anything but picked up the broom and started sweeping again.

"Have you made plans for dinner yet, Ginny?"

Ginny's broom stopped in midair. "Dinner? Tonight? No, I hadn't really thought about it."

"Let me take you out to eat."

"Oh, you don't need to do that, Honey."

"I know I don't need to, but I'd like to." Maddie put a hand on Ginny's arm. "Please? Have you eaten at the new deli yet?"

"No, I haven't. I've been wanting to try it, though. Well, all right. What time did you want to go?"

"How about six o'clock?"

"Sounds great. Just toot your horn when you're ready to leave. I'll meet you in the drive." Ginny resumed sweeping, and Maddie imagined there was a livelier lilt in her friend's step.

~~~

"Well, I hate to admit it, but this chicken noodle soup is almost as good as my own," Ginny said, dipping into her bowl for another spoonful of the rich broth as they sat across from one another in a cozy booth at the Main Street Deli. "You were right to recommend it."

Maddie smiled as she buttered a slice of wheat toast. "Well, yours must be wonderful then." An idea leapt into her brain, and she gave it voice without thinking. "Ginny, you should take some of your soup to Mr. Tyler. That ought to cure what ails him." It was the perfect overture for Ginny to make, the very opening Maddie had been seeking to get the two together. She didn't tell her neighbor that she'd already taken Arthur Tyler some of the deli's soup.

Ginny nodded, a sparkle lighting her eyes. "Maybe I'll just do that. You could take it to him when you go tomorrow."

Maddie's head came up. "Well. . .actually, I thought I might not go back. . .as long as he's not feeling well. I don't want to disturb him. But you could go and—"

"Oh, nonsense!" Ginny said. "If you come bearing food, he certainly can't complain. Besides, I'd say it's high time you two met."
~~~

Feeling caught in a trap she'd set herself, Maddie didn't argue.

~~~

Ginny phoned early Tuesday morning to say she'd been asked to help with a funeral dinner at the church, and Arthur Tyler's chicken soup would have to wait a day. Grateful for the reprieve, Maddie spent the morning at home doing laundry and tidying up the house as best she could with the tile layers working in the kitchen.

That done, she called her editor in New York to discuss a couple questions that had come up as she was writing. Janice was talkative and enthusiastic about Maddie's ideas, and Maddie hung up feeling encouraged. She had to admit it was rather nice to take a day off from writing. Her story still perked quietly in the back of her mind, and she had a feeling that when she got back to her computer the words would flow readily.

Maddie spent the afternoon sitting with her mother in the nursing home's large sunroom. At the opposite end of the room, two elderly men carried on a loud discussion. Mom seemed as oblivious to their noise as she was to Maddie's presence, but at least she wasn't agitated or uncooperative. Maddie had brought her mother's Bible and read quietly to her from the worn volume.

She didn't know if Mom understood or even heard
~~~

the words anymore, but Maddie had discovered that the Scriptures often seemed to calm her mother when she was restless.

Turning to 1 Corinthians 13, she began to read aloud. The verses seemed especially poignant today. Her throat tightened, and she felt tears well behind her eyelids. Mom didn't seem to notice, so she read on. " 'But when the perfect comes, the partial will be done away. When I was a child, I used to speak as a child, think as a child, reason as a child; when I became a man, I did away with childish things. For now we see in a mirror dimly, but then face to face; now I know in part, but then I shall know fully just as I also have been fully known.' "

Was this how it was for Mom? Seeing the world as if through a dim mirror? Yet the writer of the passage was saying that Maddie's own vision was dark compared to what it would be when she saw Jesus face-to-face. Mom's mind had been ravaged by a horrible disease, yet her spirit waited for release, waited to soar the heavens with her Savior. It was an amazing thought, and one that lifted Maddie's spirit considerably.

" 'But now abide faith, hope, love, these three; but the greatest of these is love.' "

Maddie closed the Bible and patted her mother's cold hand. "I love you, Mom."

They sat together in silence for a long while, and Maddie tried to enjoy simply being in her mother's presence.

Shortly before five, a white-uniformed nurse's aide appeared in the wide doorway. "Mrs. Houser? Are you ready to go to the dining room?"

Mom fingered the crocheted hem of her sweater, not looking up. Maddie put a hand gently on her mother's chin and tilted her head, trying to get her attention. "Mom? It's time for dinner. Shall we go to the dining room?" Mom looked into her eyes but obviously didn't recognize her. Maddie dismissed the nurse's aide with a little wave. "Thank you. I'll walk down with her."

Taking the frail hands in hers, Maddie stood and gently pulled her mother up beside her. With Maddie struggling to match the shuffling gait Alzheimer's had bestowed on her mother, they started down the long corridor together.

nine

Before the workmen arrived the next morning, Maddie heard Ginny's cheery greeting sail through the back door on the tail of her familiar knock. The hearty aroma of chicken broth wafted through the house, and Maddie followed the scent into the kitchen, where she met her guest.

"Well, good morning," Ginny said. She set the pot of soup on a dish towel on the kitchen table and looked around the room, taking in the newly laid tile floor and the partially installed faux granite countertops. "This is coming along nicely," she said.

"I'm beginning to believe there might be light at the end of the tunnel." Maddie walked across the room and ran her hand over the smooth surface of the countertop. "The guy who's doing the counters can't get back to edge them until next week, but he thought he could finish the job in a couple of days; and then the only thing left is the wallpaper border Kate picked out—that, and some touch-up painting."

"And then you won't need to go to the inn anymore. I suppose it'll be a relief not to have to lug your entire office back and forth every day."

"Yes, I suppose it will," Maddie said, surprised at how gloomy the thought made her feel. Maybe after she got the new kitchen cleaned up and all her dishes put away, she'd think differently. But when exactly was she going to find the time to do all that?

"I'd better let you get going," Ginny said, giving the soup pot a proprietary pat. "Tell Arthur all he needs to do is put this on the stove until it's warm. I don't want him boiling all the flavor away. Or maybe you could heat it up for him, Maddie? Help yourself to a bowl."

Ginny turned when she got to the back door, a wily glint sparking in her eyes. "There's plenty there for both of you. You could have lunch together."

"Oh, well. . .thank you, Ginny. I'm sure Mr. Tyler will appreciate it," Maddie said, trying to hide her dismay. If Ginny kept this up, Maddie would soon be spoon-feeding the old gentleman.

Her neighbor flapped her hands like a mother hen directing chicks. "Go on now. Don't let me keep you."

Maddie watched Ginny go out the door and bustle across the yard. Sighing, she gathered up her things, loaded the pot of soup into the car, and headed out of town. When she turned onto Hampton Road a few minutes later, she wondered what in the world she'd gotten herself into.

~~~

Arthur Tyler heard a car on the driveway and sat up in bed, disoriented. He'd tossed and turned all night long—burning up one minute and quaking with chills the next. He reached for a tissue on the nightstand and blew his nose. This bug he'd caught had laid him lower than he could remember being in a long time, but it seemed his fever had finally broken.

The gravel crunched, and Art heard the car come to a stop. Madeleine Houser must have decided to come, after all. He swung his legs over the side of the bed and went out to the kitchenette to heat some water for coffee. He wished he'd gotten up in time to brew a pot of coffee upstairs before she'd arrived.

He went to the daylight window overlooking the drive. Expecting to see Ms. Houser's old Buick in the drive, he was surprised to see a white Mazda. Someone was moving around inside the vehicle, but no one was getting out yet. He'd seen that car before. Recently. He tried to think where. Who would be coming out to the inn?

His heart lurched. Had he scheduled guests for today and forgotten about it? Pulling on a pair of blue jeans, he flew up the stairs to the main floor. He went to the desk in the parlor where he kept the appointment calendar. His
~~~

head pounded as he flipped through the bookings, trying to remember what day it was. There it was. Tuesday. No guests were scheduled until the weekend.

The sound of a key turning in the front door mere feet from where he stood caused his heart to race even faster. That would be Madeleine Houser. Strange, he hadn't heard another car drive in. Glancing up at the antique mirror that hung over the parlor desk, he caught sight of his reflection. *Good grief.* He would frighten the poor woman to death! Two days' worth of black stubble sprouted from his jawline, his hair spiked out in forty different directions, and his nose would give Rudolph a run for his money.

Art clapped the appointment book shut and raced back through the house, practically diving down the staircase to his apartment. Out of breath, his heart thumping in his ears, he draped himself over a bar stool in the downstairs kitchenette and leaned against the counter. The front door closed, and quiet footsteps echoed from the hall above him.

A repeat of Monday morning's litany of sounds began—a computer being turned on, water running into a carafe. Soon the coffeemaker was chugging and hissing. Today, Art's sinuses were considerably less stuffy, and the delicious aroma tickled his nose.

He listened as the footsteps retreated through the house and out the front door. She must have left something in the car. Curious, Art went to the window and watched.

He didn't see Ms. Houser's Buick, but the white Mazda was still parked in the driveway. The driver—a woman—had gotten out and was bent over, taking something from the backseat.

A brisk breeze kicked up, and she struggled to hold the car door open with one knee while she tugged on something in the car. Finally she stood and turned to face the house, holding a large cooking dish of some sort in her hands. The wind whipped her dark blond hair in her face, and she flipped her head back, trying unsuccessfully to shake the thick mane out of her eyes. She turned slightly and gave the car door a shove with one hip—one very shapely hip, Arthur couldn't help but notice. She turned and started up the front walk, casserole dish in hand.

Art watched until she disappeared from his line of vision. Something clicked in his brain. His heart stopped beating, and his next breath came in a tight wheeze. The white Mazda. Of course! That's where he'd seen it. It was the woman from the post office—the lovely Miss Green Eyes. Coming up his walk. What in the world was she doing here? And why was she bringing food?

He wasn't about to answer the door. Where was Madeleine Houser? He thought he'd heard her go outside just moments ago. Maybe she would tell Green Eyes that he was indisposed. Wait. Maybe Green Eyes was a friend of Madeleine Houser. Maybe she'd brought the food for the author. He looked out on the drive again. The Buick was nowhere to be seen. Had the author left already? But why would she set up her computer, make coffee, and then leave? It didn't make sense. Unless she'd forgotten something and run home for it.

Art listened for the doorbell. Instead, he heard the front door open and the floorboards above him creak. He leaned against the wall that concealed the stairway. He heard the refrigerator open and close, the sound of coffee being poured, and soon the steady click of a computer keyboard. What was going on?

Alex slipped past him and ran up the steps.

"Well, hello there, Alex," a familiar voice cooed. "Are you being a bad boy again? You're going to get me in trouble, you know. Now you go on. Get back down there and keep Mr. Tyler's feet warm."

Slowly, as though Art Tyler had been a horse wearing blinders and his master had finally slipped the offending apparatus from his eyes, the puzzle started falling into place.

Tyler, you idiot! How could you be so dumb?

A thought pierced his mind, and he hurried into the bedroom and threw open Annie's side of the closet. Annabeth's sister and nieces had helped him pack up Annie's clothes and shoes more than a year ago, but two shelves in the back of the closet still held part of her beloved collection of books. Art knelt in front of the shelves and ran his fingers along the titles, looking almost frantically for one particular volume.

There it was. *Hope's Song* by Madeleine Houser.

Art slipped the book from the shelf, somehow knowing what he would find even before he opened the cover. He turned the book over, opened to the back flap of the dust jacket, and stared at the photograph.

A familiar pair of mesmerizing green eyes stared back at him.

The beautiful young woman at the post office—the one who'd made his heart beat a little faster—was Madeleine Houser. Green Eyes was the author of the compelling novel in which he'd immersed himself for the past few nights. Green Eyes was Ginny's friend. That lovely creature was the one who'd penned the delightful notes Art had so looked forward to each evening. She had spent the past month in this very house—his house!

As each revelation came to him, it boggled his mind all over again. How could his perceptions have been so ridiculously wrong? What happened to the gray-haired old lady? The one who walked with a cane and drove an old monster of a Buick?

Why hadn't Ginny *told* him? But what had there been to tell? Ginny couldn't know that he was infatuated with the lovely stranger at the post office. He looked at Madeleine Houser's publicity photo on the book jacket again. If he had taken Ginny's advice, he would have read one of Ms. Houser's books and put two and two together long ago.

Art fell back on the floor against the bed and sat with his head in his hands, laughing softly to himself as each intricate facet of this great deception—one he'd apparently manufactured with his own mind—came to light.

Twenty minutes later, he felt a brush of soft fur against his bare arm. "Hey, Alex. You rascal. You knew all along, didn't you?" He chuckled quietly and scratched the cat under the chin, shaking his head.

A wry grin tugging at one corner of his mouth, Arthur Tyler finally hauled himself off the floor and went down the hall to the shower. It was time to clean up and properly introduce himself to the lovely and talented—and ever so young—Madeleine Houser.

~~~

Maddie heard the sound of running water downstairs. Mr. Tyler must be up and around. Maybe he'd come upstairs and she could offer to warm some of Ginny's soup for him. That ought to make her neighbor happy.

She felt rather excited and just a bit nervous at the prospect of finally meeting her mysterious host—and the hero of her novel. But of course she wouldn't tell him about that. A flush of heat crept up her neck at the mere thought.

She saved her latest chapter to the computer's hard drive and went into the kitchen to put Ginny's soup on to
~~~

heat. If Mr. Tyler didn't come up, maybe she'd get up the courage to take a bowl down to him. Compliments of Ginny, of course.

She found a package of soup crackers in a basket on top of the refrigerator and fixed a tray with a cloth napkin and a glass of ice water. On a whim, she went out to the front porch and plucked one of the faded roses from the bush in front of the house. She put it in a tiny bud vase she'd found on the open shelves in the kitchen. Surveying her handiwork with satisfaction, she stirred the soup once more and listened for sounds of life in the apartment downstairs.

The water had stopped running, but all was quiet below. Maybe he'd gone back to bed. She certainly didn't want to wake him. Not sure what she should do, Maddie turned the heat down under the soup and went back to try to write another scene in her novel.

A few unproductive minutes later, Alex's meow caused her to look up from her computer. Footsteps sounded on the stairway not ten feet from where she sat. Ah, he *was* awake. She was finally going to meet the elusive Arthur Tyler. She sat up straighter in her chair. Quickly slipping off her glasses, she moistened her lips and tucked her hair behind her ears.

But the head that appeared over the railing did not belong to Arthur Tyler. It was. . .it was the lawn guy. The man from the post office. Maddie took in a sharp breath, mildly alarmed that he had just walked into the house.

"Oh! Hello," she said, trying not to appear frightened. She pushed back her chair and stood, glad the massive oak table sat between them. "I'm Madeleine Houser. You must be here to mow the lawn. I–I saw you working in the yard the other day," she explained, motioning toward the front of the house.

The man stared at her as though she were making no sense whatsoever.

"Um. . .Mr. Tyler is home sick today," she explained. "He's downstairs. I–I can get him if you like."

The man's bemused gaze made her extremely uncomfortable.

"Madeleine?"

Maddie swallowed hard. How did he know her name? And today wasn't Friday, the day Mr. Tyler usually had the lawn mowed. Maddie's heart began to beat erratically.

The man came up the last two stairs to the landing, and Maddie took a step back, bumping into the chair behind her.

He put a hand to his chest. "Ms. Houser, *I'm* Arthur Tyler."

"Wh–what?" What kind of nut case was this guy?

"I'm sorry if I frightened you," he said, shaking his head. "I thought you knew I was home sick today. I–I don't think I'm contagious anymore. I just thought it was time I introduced myself." He waited, looking at her with a spark of amusement in his eyes.

"You're Arthur Tyler? But I thought. . ."

"Yes, I'm Art Tyler. You thought I was someone else?"

Maddie reached behind her, felt for the brocade seat of the straight-backed chair, and crumpled onto it. "I'm sorry. I'm. . .a little confused right now. I thought. . ." The truth began to unfold in her mind, and she giggled. "Well, I thought you were. . ."

He waited, his dark brows knit together.

She started again. "For some reason, I assumed you were Ginny's friend. Well, I know you *are* her friend, but I thought you were Ginny's age. I thought you were *old.*" She knew she was rambling like a tumbleweed in a twister, but her brain was having trouble wrapping itself around the obvious truth.

Arthur Tyler threw back his head and laughed. "You thought *I* was old?" he said, when he finally caught his breath. "I thought the same thing!"

"You thought you were old?" Maybe he *was* a nut case after all.

He laughed again. "No, no. I thought *you* were old. Ginny said she had this writer friend and I just jumped to—"

"Apparently we both jumped to some conclusions," Maddie said, her mind whirling, trying desperately to sort out this whole outrageous scenario.

"Yes," Arthur said, a hint of suspicion creeping into his voice, "and I don't recall our friend Ginny doing anything to correct those misperceptions."

Maddie thought for a minute, remembering the mischievous gleam in Ginny's eye earlier that morning. "You're right. I'm sure I said something that would have led her to believe—wait a minute! And to think I was trying to—" She blushed and stopped herself.

"What?"

Maddie giggled again. "I was trying to set you and Ginny up. I thought she had a crush on you. But all this time—"

Arthur Tyler took a step toward her, and a light of recognition came to his eyes—eyes that up close were exactly the shade of blue gray Maddie had imagined.

"Ginny Ross was trying to set *us* up? Is that it?" he asked.

Maddie smiled and nodded slowly, remembering her neighbor's insistence that Maddie deliver the chicken soup in person. "I have a feeling that's exactly what she was up to."

Arthur pulled a chair out from the dining room table, turned it around, and straddled it, resting his arms on the high back. "Well, isn't that one for the books?"

They sat looking at one another, smiling wordlessly. Finally Arthur unfolded his lean body from the chair, rose, and stretched out a hand. "Madeleine Houser, I'm Arthur Tyler. I'm very pleased to finally meet you. The *real* you."

Maddie took his hand, smiling broadly. "And I'm

pleased to meet you, too, kind sir. After all our correspondence, I–I wish I could say, 'I feel like I know you,' but I'm so confused right now, I'm afraid that wouldn't be altogether true."

"No." He laughed. "Not for me, either." He dipped his head. "But I'd certainly like to remedy that."

She smiled softly and nodded, savoring the warmth of his hand clasped tightly over hers.

ten

The kitchen smelled of chicken broth and coffee and the slightest hint of some delicate, feminine cologne. After being without his olfactory senses for several days, Arthur Tyler inhaled each scent with fresh appreciation.

He smiled at the woman sitting across from him and spooned another bite of the steaming soup into his mouth. "Mmm. . .this is wonderful," he said over a mouthful of noodles. "I think I feel better already. I can see why they say this stuff has medicinal value," he added, quoting a recent communiqué from his dining companion.

"Well, I'd say this goes down a bit easier than medicine." Madeleine Houser dabbed daintily at the corner of her mouth with a paper napkin.

For a few moments the two ate together in silence—a remarkably comfortable silence, given the fact they'd met only some twenty minutes ago.

Yet watching her, Art felt he knew the soul of the

beautiful woman sitting at his table. His heart swelled at the amazing discoveries they'd made, and he wondered what other surprises God had in store for them. To think they'd each had such skewed perceptions of the other. Every time he remembered the comedy of errors that had brought them to this moment, he wanted to laugh out loud.

Madeleine looked up and caught him watching her, but the quirk of her shapely lips told him she was having similar thoughts.

"So all this time you've imagined me as a doddering old man?"

"Not exactly doddering," she said, tilting her head. "I was thinking more along the lines of distinguished and. . .dapper."

Art watched with delight as a blush of crimson climbed her throat.

"I wish I could give parallel adjectives for the picture I had of Ms. Madeleine Houser, elderly author. But the truth is, I thought you were just plain *old*."

"Hey!" She shot him a look that was exactly what he'd aimed for.

He cocked his head to one side and held up a finger. "Ah, but let's talk about my opinion of the mysterious woman at the post office."

"Let's not," she protested. But her smile very clearly said the opposite.

He turned serious. "May I ask what you were so upset about that day—in the car?"

Madeleine put her spoon down and thought for a minute, then giggled like a schoolgirl.

"What?" He leaned forward, his curiosity piqued.

She put an elbow on the table and rested her chin on one hand. "I was in tears because my proofreader had just returned my manuscript with a note saying she was quitting."

"Oh. . ." One more piece of the puzzle plunked into place. "Well, hey, didn't you tell me that one day you'd probably be able to laugh about it?"

She convulsed with giggles. Art was quickly growing to love the sound of her laughter.

Her amusement subsided and a wistful note came to her voice. "I really didn't expect that day to come quite so soon."

"I'm so glad it did."

She rewarded him with a smile. "Me, too."

"Your book is wonderful, Madeleine—may I call you Madeleine?" It felt right, but he wanted to be certain.

"My friends call me Maddie."

He nodded. "Then Maddie it is. And I mean it. Your book is excellent."

"Thank you, Arthur—"

"Please, my friends call me Art."

"Art, then." She bobbed her chin and grinned up at him. "I was nervous. . .about having you read it."

"What? You, nervous about some old geezer's opinion?"

"I'd grown to like that old geezer quite a bit. And to respect his opinion." A mischievous glimmer came to her eyes. "Frankly I'm not sure I can take the critique of a young whippersnapper like you seriously."

Art laughed until the tears came. If he'd believed in love at first sight, he would have dropped to one knee and declared his love for this woman on the spot. But he managed to restrain himself and simply enjoy her clever wit.

Maddie. Yes, the name fit Green Eyes perfectly.

She jumped up and went to the kitchen, came back with a pitcher of water, and refilled his glass.

"Thank you. You don't have to wait on me, you know."

"I don't mind. You're not feeling well. Besides, I can never begin to repay you for allowing me to take over your house like this."

"Speaking of which," he said, balling up his napkin and pushing back his chair, "I need to let you get back to work." He gathered up their bowls and spoons and carried them into the kitchen. Poking his head back into the dining room, he added, "Pretend I'm not here. I'll get these dishes washed up. You get back to that story."

She stood and picked up their drinking glasses. "No. . . really, let me take care of them. It won't take a minute."

Art met her at the table and put a hand on her arm, gently taking the dishes from her. "I'm not taking no for an answer. Please."

"Well. . .thank you." She sat back down.

He went back to the kitchen and ran the sink full of hot water. While he washed dishes, he listened to the rhythmic *tap, tap, tap* of her computer keyboard. He was just wiping off the counters when he heard her gasp.

He hurried out to the dining room to find her sitting, mouth agape, staring at her computer.

"What is it? Is everything all right?"

She turned slowly to stare at him, her eyes glazed over. "You're my hero."

"Excuse me? Just because I did the dishes?" This woman must have had some bad experiences with men.

"No! You're my hero," she repeated, looking him in the eye. "The photograph upstairs. That's you!"

He waited, dish towel in hand, as an expression he couldn't quite read swept over her lovely features.

"I just figured something out."

"Would you care to tell me?" Art smiled. "Or would you rather write me a note?"

She gave him a crooked smile and dipped her head. "I saw the photograph upstairs of you and your wife. The old-fashioned one. I thought it was you—when you were young—" She giggled, then shook her head. "This is very complicated."

He waited, rather enjoying her discomfort.

"I needed a face for my hero and. . .well, I borrowed yours. I hope you don't mind."

Art curbed a grin. "No wonder I liked Jonathan Barlowe so well."

Maddie laughed again and turned a luscious shade of

pink. But Art was flattered at the implication.

"Ginny said your wife. . .Annabeth. . .died," Maddie added quietly.

His breath caught at the sound of Annie's name, but the sympathy in Maddie's voice touched a place deep within him. "Yes." He looked at the floor. "Cancer. It will have been three years next April."

"I'm so sorry. She was very beautiful."

He nodded, unable to speak. Suddenly desperate to change the subject, he moved toward the stairway. "I'm keeping you from your work," he said. "I'd better get back downstairs."

"Oh, no." She scooted her chair back from the table. "I'm not going to kick you out of your own dining room. I'll go now. I can come back when you've returned to work."

"Please. Don't go, Maddie. I needed to get busy anyway. I have papers to grade downstairs."

"Well. . .if you're sure. . ."

"Positive." He smiled and stretched out a hand again. "Madeleine—"

She took it, and the pink in her cheeks blossomed.

"It was very nice to finally meet you."

"You, too. . .Arthur."

He went slowly down the steps. Retrieving a stack of freshman essays from his briefcase, he took the papers to the eating bar in the kitchen and tried to concentrate on marking them. But thoughts of Annie flitted through his mind. More than once, the music of feminine laughter floated down the stairway, and he knew that Green Eyes was remembering some little incident, some little providential twist of timing that had led to their meeting today.

This house had been a long time without a woman's laughter.

eleven

The next morning when Maddie emerged from the steamy bathroom, hair still damp from her shower, a blinking light on the answering machine told her she had a message. She listened to it while she did her makeup.

"Hello, Maddie. It's Art. Just wanted to let you know Ginny's soup worked its magic and I'm going back to work today, so the house is all yours. Please make yourself at home. I–I've left you a note. . .in the usual place. Well. . .that's all. Bye now."

A twinge of guilt accompanied the thrill that went up her spine at the sound of Art's voice. But she detected a note of hesitancy in his voice, too, and wondered what it meant. She'd dreamed of Arthur Tyler—Art—both waking and sleeping since she'd left the inn yesterday. She had fallen and fallen hard. But did she even know the man? Or was she in love with the idea of being in love?

"What are you talking about, Houser?" she chided,

looking her reflection in the eye as she ran a brush through her hair. She stopped, hairbrush in midstroke. "You don't know what love is." But, oh, how she wanted to.

Sitting across from Art over chicken noodle soup yesterday, talking, laughing together, it had seemed as though they were old, dear friends. And she did know something of his heart—his dreams and desires—from the notes they'd exchanged over the last few weeks. She sighed. In a way, they'd been courting since the second day she went to the inn and found his thoughtful note in reply to hers. They just hadn't realized it.

Maddie wondered what Art was feeling this morning. Had he sensed the connection as strongly as she? Even though his wife had been gone for several years, it was obvious from his reaction yesterday that he was still reeling from that loss. She would need to tread lightly.

With a nest of butterflies in her stomach, she drove out to the inn, feeling a new kind of anticipation over the note that waited. She let herself in and hurried to the dining room. Without bothering to set up her computer, she picked up the sheet of paper on the table.

As she read, her heart dipped and soared and dipped again like a kite in a frivolous March wind.

Dear Maddie,

Not Ms. Houser, not Madeleine, but dear Maddie. I'm still trying to sort out all the crazy misunderstandings that kept us from meeting until yesterday. But somehow I know it was for the best. I think perhaps if we'd met that first day you came to write at the inn, we never would have grown to know and respect one another as we have. (At least I hope you share those feelings with me.)

I suppose you need to know that I've put up some walls where women—especially beautiful, talented, available women—are concerned. My marriage was an extremely happy one, but it had a tragic ending. And since you and I have been honest with one another from the start, I'll tell you that I have a tremendous fear that I will never be able to love that way again. I don't want you to expect what I'm not sure I can give.

Perhaps I am seriously premature in sharing these things with you—and now in making a request—but what I said yesterday was true: I would like to get to know you better. Could we have dinner again, soon? A real—dare I say it—date? If I've misread your interest, please be honest with me, and please forgive me. But if not, what does this coming Saturday night look like on your calendar? The college symphony is performing, and I have two tickets. (And someone told me about a wonderful new restaurant that just opened in Wichita. We could eat before the concert.)

I admit that I'm a little nervous about this next step in our friendship. Frankly I adored the elderly, charming, "safe" Madeleine Houser; and I'm a little sad to think that she's gone from my life. But I have a feeling her younger counterpart will win me over just as quickly. In fact, I'm not sure that she hasn't already.

I'll hope to find your response when I get home tonight, but if you need to think it over for a while, I will understand.

Your friend,
Art

Maddie read the note again, caressing the smooth paper between her thumb and forefinger. How was she supposed to finish her novel, make her deadline, *breathe,* when the letter she held in her hands contained such undisguised hesitancy—such fragile promise?

She read the note a third time and found herself more confused than ever. What did the man want? First it seemed as if he were making romantic overtures, but then he held out a warning that no one could fill the place Annie had in his heart. Yet in his very next breath he was asking her for a date. Did the man have a clue what he wanted? Did he care that he was stringing her along like some kind of puppet?

She picked up her pen and turned over Art's note,

ready to write her reply on the back. But she didn't want to part with this paper. She needed to take it home and read it again, attempt to decipher the true message his words held.

Digging in her computer bag, she found a legal pad; but she sat for several minutes, pen poised, mind reeling, before she knew what she wanted to say.

Dear Art,

Rest assured, I am every bit as frightened and uncertain as you are. Having said that, my calendar is free for Saturday, and I can't think of a more pleasant way to spend it than at dinner and the symphony with a friend.

Shall we keep it at that, with no other expectations or potential? Just friends? I could use a friend right now.

Maddie

She capped the pen and laid it on the table. She understood what Art meant about being sad to see the imagined, elderly friend go. She felt the same about Arthur Tyler. With "old Mr. Tyler," she'd never had to measure her words so carefully. Never had to worry that she would be judged by him the way men her age judged women.

Had they ruined the wonderful friendship they'd shared by the simple act of being introduced? Did the mere fact that they were the same age, and therefore eligible for romance with one another, doom their friendship? A mirthless laugh escaped her lips. This surely broke her track record for destroying a relationship. Friends to strangers almost before she met the guy.

She set up her computer, opened the file to her manuscript, and forced herself to start typing when what she really wanted was to put her head in her hands and weep.

~~~

Art sat in Ginny Ross's cozy living room, sipping tea from a flowery china cup. He feared he might snap the handle from the fragile vessel merely by picking it up. They'd discussed global news and local politics, and now they'd worked their way down to the weather.

Beside him on the slipcovered sofa, Ginny set her own teacup on the doily strewn coffee table. "Well, enough small talk. What did you really come here for, Arthur?"

Art smiled. Ginny had never been one to mince words. Okay, he would follow her lead, lay it all out for her, and see if she had a cure for his jumbled emotions. "I think I'm in love with your neighbor."

Ginny hooked a thumb to the north and feigned shock. "Elma Wheaton? I don't know, Art. She's awfully old for you, don't you think?"

"Very funny, Ginny. You know exactly who I mean."
~~~

He sobered. "I think I'm in love with Madeleine Houser."

Ginny's expression was unreadable. "So why are you telling *me?* Seems Madeleine ought to be the first to hear this startling announcement."

"She already has. . .well, sort of."

"Arthur, how do you 'sort of' tell a woman you love her? Seems to me either you do or you don't."

"Ginny—"

The elderly woman's eyes softened, and she reached over to pat his knee. "It's Annie, isn't it?"

Art put his head in his hands, grateful that Ginny had guessed. "I know it's not right, Ginny. I know it, but I don't know what to do about it."

"Art, Annie's not coming back. Ever. I know you understand that," she said gently. "And I know Annie wanted you to go on with your life."

Tears were close to the surface, but he held them at bay. "I'm just. . .so afraid that no one will ever be able to compare to her. We had such a good thing, Ginny. Right up until the end—a *perfect* thing and—"

"No, it *wasn't* perfect, Art." Ginny wagged her head. "My memory sometimes tends to gloss over the bad times Grover and I had, too. But that wouldn't be right. It wouldn't be honest. Oh, it was mostly good, just as it was for you and Annie. But don't forget the struggles, Art. Don't romanticize them. That's not fair—not to Annie and certainly not to Madeleine."

Art thought about what Ginny had said. Yes, if he stretched his memory, he could acknowledge that he and Annie had sometimes fought. But they'd never let the sun go down on their anger. They'd never hurt each other beyond forgiveness. Oh, it was nothing he could take credit for. It was all Annie. Her spirit had been ever gentle and loving even after she became so ill.

He turned to Ginny, feeling like a child, yet grateful he could pour out his fears to someone older and wiser. "What if. . .what if I marry someone else and it's not as good as it was with Annie? I know what marriage is meant to be. I can't risk ruining the memories I have."

Ginny leaned in and took both his hands in hers. Her frail, veined hands were dwarfed by his own, but there was surprising strength in her grasp.

She gave his hands a little shake that made him look her in the eye. "Arthur Tyler, I know you well enough to know that you, of all people, are not going to do anything to sully the institution of marriage. Oh, if you're putting your faith in yourself, maybe. But I know you better than that. You've always been one to trust God for your life. Why are you withholding this one thing?"

"I–I guess I didn't realize that I was."

"Well, I'm here to tell you that you are."

He didn't reply. He didn't need to.

Ginny let go of his hands, giving each a final pat, then pushed herself off the sofa. "I'm going to make some more tea. You want some?"

He nodded, grateful to be left alone with his thoughts.

~~~

Art looped one end of his necktie over the other and tied the knot unconsciously. The man staring back at him from the mirror certainly didn't *look* riddled with guilt. He wished they could trade places.

He knew it was wrong for him to feel this way. Annie had been gone for a long time. And besides, Ginny was right: Annie had given her blessing for him to find love again. At the time, he'd resented it, still being in denial, refusing to believe that God would ever take his Annie from him. For a long time after her death, her blessing was meaningless, since he'd had no desire to so much as look at another woman.

But now there was a living, breathing woman who had stolen into his life under cover of acute misunderstanding, and he'd fallen in love almost without realizing it. Okay, maybe it was a bit of a stretch to call it love. He didn't really know her. Yet he felt he did. The notes they'd shared had opened windows into each of their hearts. And now having met Maddie, having discovered that they shared much more than he'd ever imagined, he could not deny that she made his heart pump to a rhythm he'd long forgotten—one that was all too familiar.
~~~

Tuesday he had sat across the table from a beautiful woman and for the first time since Annabeth McGee, he'd felt that enthralling pull on his heartstrings. It had energized him like nothing had in a very long time.

Now four days later, that tug on his heart had become a tug-of-war. And right now, guilt was pulling far more weight on the rope of his emotions. Luckily, Maddie didn't appear to be as smitten as he was. In truth, his heart had sunk when he'd read her note. She seemed determined to remain friends and nothing more. But perhaps that was a good thing.

Then there was the matter of their date. *No,* he mentally corrected himself, *their evening together*. If she only wanted to be friends, he had to quit thinking of tonight as a date. Maddie was probably dressing for the evening this very minute. He wondered how she would look all dressed up.

Stop it, Tyler. She's a friend. That's all. These thoughts were hardly appropriate toward a woman who was just a friend. But he couldn't help it. An image of her smooth, pale hair and those tantalizing green eyes popped into his mind. He could almost hear the melody of her laughter.

He was going to drive himself insane thinking this way. With a sharp tug, he finished his tie, checked his pockets for the symphony tickets, and headed out to the pickup. He drove into town, perspiring—in spite of the fact that the temperature had dipped below thirty.

twelve

Maddie paced the living room, making occasional forays into the bathroom to check her lipstick, add one last spritz of hair spray, and adjust the collar of her white silk blouse.

It wasn't often that she got to dress up, and it had been rather fun to go all out this evening. She just hoped she hadn't overdone it. She didn't want Arthur to get the wrong idea.

The front doorbell chimed. Maddie's breath caught in her throat. She rubbed damp palms on her long velvet skirt as she walked through the house to the living room. Putting her hand on the doorknob, she took a deep breath and opened the door.

Art stood in front of her, handsome in a dark suit with a tie the same shade of blue as his eyes. "Hi, Maddie. You. . .look lovely." He was almost stuttering; and Maddie felt certain, looking into the deep pools of those eyes, that it wasn't the appreciation of a mere friend that she saw there.

"You clean up pretty nice, too," she teased, determined to keep things light and friendly.

"Are you ready to go?"

"Yes, let me just get my coat." She hurried into the bedroom and came back with a silk paisley jacket over her arm. "Okay, all ready," she said, nerves taut.

Art led the way down the front walk and went around to open the door for her. It was a bit of a climb to get up into his pickup, but she managed to do so with a reasonable measure of grace. He carefully tucked the hem of her skirt out of harm's way before closing the door and coming around to the driver's seat.

They were silent while Art navigated the tree-lined streets to the edge of town. He merged easily into the flow of traffic on the interstate and set the cruise control, then turned to Maddie. "I got to thinking that the university's symphony is going to seem pretty Podunk to you—compared to the concerts you've probably heard in New York, I mean."

She waved off his warning. "It's been so long since I've been to a concert that I think I'd enjoy a kindergarten kazoo band at this point."

"That's good," he laughed, "because that may be exactly what this group sounds like to your ears."

"Art, I'm really not the connoisseur of music you paint me to be. I do love classical music, but I'm no critic."

"Well, we'll see after tonight," he said, flashing a wry grin.

For the rest of the drive into Wichita, they talked animatedly about music and movies and books they'd enjoyed. In the space of an hour, she successfully eliminated her earlier image of Art as a distinguished, elderly professor and replaced it with the witty, handsome, flesh-and-blood man seated behind the wheel of this Chevy 4x4—an exchange she made gladly.

Art asked her about her writing career and gave a glowing critique of her work in progress. "I'm not finished yet, of course, but what I've read so far is beautifully done. I will truly feel guilty if you pay me to proofread this, Maddie."

"Well, if you won't let me pay you, then you'd better quit reading right now, because I'm already so indebted to you for the use of the inn that I'll never get out of hock."

"Hey," he said lightly, "can we come to some sort of understanding about this? We both feel we're cheating the other, so let's just call it even and not bring it up again."

"I like that plan," she said, laughing.

They ate at a new Italian place on the east side of town. Dinner brought more pleasant conversation. Again, Maddie had the sense that she'd known Art forever.

And later, in spite of Art's caveat, Maddie thoroughly enjoyed the concert. The small symphony was quite accomplished, and Maddie's favorite concertos were on the program. She was sorry when it was over. On the way out the door, Art purchased one of the CDs the group had for sale, and they listened to it on the drive home.

"You know," she said, as strains of Mendelssohn threaded around them, "when I saw this pickup truck, I was just sure we'd be listening to country music all the way."

Art smiled. "I like to keep people guessing."

Boy, does he have that *right.*

"Actually, I do listen to country occasionally," he said. "I like the stories those songs tell—ballads, I guess they're called. But there's just something timeless about the classics."

"Did your wife. . .did Annie like classical music?" Maddie ventured. There was an overlong silence before he replied. For a minute, remembering Art's quick exit the last time the topic of Annabeth came up, Maddie was afraid she'd stepped on sacred ground. Still, she wanted him to know that, for her anyway, the subject of Annie didn't have to be off-limits.

"Yes, she did like music," Art said finally. "Annie played the piano beautifully and always had Mozart or Vivaldi going on the stereo." He took one hand off the steering wheel and turned toward her a bit. "Do you play? Piano?"

She cringed and shook her head. "Only for my own enjoyment. I mostly play by ear—by heart, Mom calls it. Well. . .called it." She looked at her lap, then swallowed hard and attempted to inject some levity into her voice. "I would never inflict my pathetic attempts on an audience."

"I'm sure you play beautifully."

"It's cheap therapy. I'm out of practice, though. My sister's piano is desperately out of tune, and I left my baby grand in storage in New York."

"Are you going back?" he asked abruptly. "To New York, I mean. Is Clayton temporary?"

She sighed. "I honestly don't know. My mom is only sixty-three. She could live for many years. I want to be there for her."

Art reached out to touch her arm. "How is your mom doing?"

Maddie was moved by his concern. "She's at a fairly advanced stage of the disease. I don't think she's known who I am for quite awhile."

"I'm sorry. That must be so hard. I admire you. . .for wanting to be there for her."

"Well, I'm not doing anything heroic. But I am glad it's worked out for me to be here. And I do like Clayton. If it weren't for the house being so torn up, I couldn't really complain."

"Oh, but if it weren't for the house being torn up, you wouldn't be sitting here beside me right now. I think that was a gift."

Maddie's mind whirled. The man's words confused her as much as his note had. Well, she was just going to speak her mind. What did she have to lose? She drew herself up in the seat and formed the question in her mind.

"Art, I—"

"Maddie—"

She turned to him.

"What?" they said in unison, then both laughed softly.

"You first." He waited, curiosity evident on his face.

The butterflies began to flit again. "Art, I'm confused. I–I'm too old to play games, so I want to get this out in the open."

"Okay. . . ." His tone was understandably cautious.

She took another deep breath. "Your note the other day confused the life out of me."

He seemed surprised. "What do you mean?"

"In one breath you're asking me for a date, and in the next you're warning me that you've put up this wall because of Annie. Then you change gears again and say that I've already won you over—whatever that means." Against her will, her voice went up an octave. "The bottom line is I don't have a clue where I stand with you. I don't know if you're determined that we can never be more than friends or if you truly meant this night to be. . .a date." She suddenly felt a little foolish—and more than a bit vulnerable—for laying everything out so blatantly.

Art ran a hand through his thick hair, then put both hands back on the steering wheel and stared straight ahead for a long minute. She was afraid she'd made him angry.

When he finally spoke, his voice was so quiet she could scarcely hear it over the truck's engine. "Oh, Maddie. I'm sorry."

He reached across the seat and took her hand in his. A tiny tremor went up her spine.

His Adam's apple bobbed in his throat. "If I've confused you, it's only because I'm confused myself. I–I do want to get to know you. No. . ." He turned to meet her gaze briefly before training his eyes back on the road. "As long as we're being totally honest here, the truth is that I already feel as though I do know you and I–I like what I see, Maddie. I like it a lot. I don't just mean what I see with my eyes, although that's altogether pleasant, too."

For a moment, his eyes sought hers again, and he gave her hand a squeeze. Maddie felt the pleasure of his words warm her cheeks.

"What I really mean is that. . .well, I had a little bit of a crush on you when I thought you were eighty years old. But you were *safe* then. You weren't going to mess up the comfortable little world of grief I live in."

He waited, as though wanting a response, but she didn't know how to answer him.

"I know this sounds totally unreasonable, Maddie, but now that I've met you, I feel like I'm almost. . .I don't know. . .in love with you—which would be wonderful if that feeling weren't eating me alive with guilt."

She stared at him. Now he was in *love* with her? Talk about confused. The man was crazy! She finally found her voice. "You feel guilty because of Annie?" she whispered, wanting to make sure she understood.

He nodded, but even in the darkness of the truck's cab, he couldn't hide the emotion that tinted his face.

"Art. . ." She pulled her hand out of his warm grasp and let it fall in her lap. "I've had my heart broken enough times that I don't go seeking out that experience. There's no way I can compete with. . .with Annie. With a memory. And if you're looking for someone to ease your guilt, I'm sorry, but I don't think I'm your gal."

"I'm sorry," he said. "I'm so sorry to have put you in this awkward position. I want to be able to open my heart again. I truly do, Maddie. And I've never said that to any woman before. But. . .I don't know. I can't seem to find the way."

She stared at her lap. "Thank you for being honest with me," she said softly.

He acknowledged her words with a nod. "I'm trying, Maddie, that's all I can promise."

"I know. . .I know you are. But I don't know if my heart can take the chance that you'll fail."

They drove the rest of the way home in silence. When they got to Maddie's house, Art came around and opened her door. She rummaged frantically in her purse, looking for her keys, not wanting to create an awkward moment at the door.

She finally found them in one corner of her bag. She jangled them in front of her. "Ah, here they are. I–I'm fine now."

Art smiled, and she felt her heart respond.

"Let me walk you to the door."

"It's okay. You don't have to, Art."

"Maddie—" He scuffed the toe of his shoe in the gravel on her drive. "I don't want to sound like a broken record, but I'm sorry. I've ruined what should have been a delightful evening."

"It's okay, Art. You can't help what you feel." She made her voice bright. "I enjoyed the concert very much. And thank you for dinner. It was delicious."

"You're welcome," he said.

"Well. . .good night." She turned and started up the walk.

"Good night."

Maddie was aware of Art's pickup idling in the drive until he saw that she was safely in the house. She locked the front door behind her, flipped off the lights, and parted the curtain. She watched him back out of her driveway, then followed the taillights of his truck until they disappeared from sight. Letting the drapes fall, she put a hand over her heart in a futile effort to assuage the ache of longing there.

Art had said that he wanted to open his heart again. Well, she had done just that, and look where it had gotten her. She walked across the room to Kate's old upright piano and ran her fingers idly over the dusty keys. Their sour, metallic clang pierced the stillness. A dissonant note hung in the air, and Maddie closed her eyes. She was playing at love the way she played the piano—by heart.

thirteen

Back at the inn, Art got ready for bed. . .but sleep eluded him. Finally he crawled from beneath the covers and paced his apartment into the wee hours of the morning—thinking, praying, agonizing. The pain he'd seen in Maddie's eyes tonight broke his heart. He'd done that to her.

He wanted so desperately to put the past behind him, to offer Maddie his love with no reservations, no strings attached. But what kind of man would he be if he could let Annie go so easily?

On a whim, he went to the closet and pulled their wedding album from the top shelf. He sank to the floor at the foot of the bed and put the album in his lap. He'd nearly worn the pages out those first weeks after Annie died. But months had passed since he'd last looked at the photographs and mementos tucked inside. As he leafed through the pages, he remembered why. The vivid images caused him to remember every curve of her face, every nuance of her smile. In one shot, the camera had captured Annie's luminous face as she walked down the aisle toward him. She'd been oblivious—they both had—to the horror that would ravage their lives a short decade later.

Art turned the last page and slowly eased the cover closed. He put the album aside on the floor. Then another book caught his eye—the hardcover copy of Maddie's novel, the one that had revealed her identity to him. *Hope's Song.* He slid it from the shelf again, flipped open the back cover, and stared at her image. Judging by the book's copyright date, the photograph must have been at least four or five years old. Maddie's hair was shorter and curlier. But her smile was the same. . .as was the sparkle in her eyes.

He riffled the pages absently, deep in thought. Suddenly something caught his eye. Markings on the pages. Yellow highlighted sections and notes scribbled in Annie's handwriting. Art had scolded her a hundred times for dog-earing and highlighting and writing in their books. It had been a constant source of frustration for him. But her friends had loved to borrow her books. It was like getting a free study guide, they always said.

Art smiled wryly as he thought about what Ginny had said that afternoon. He hadn't merely rebuked Annie for what he viewed as her careless disrespect of books. He'd yelled at her. Called her irresponsible and wasteful. His academic background had caused him to hold books in high esteem, and he'd brought Annie to tears more than once over their ongoing disagreement in that department. Ginny was right. It hadn't all been a bed of roses.

He flipped through the pages of the book and read a few of Annie's cryptic marginal notes. "Echoes the theme of Pastor LeBlanc's sermon series," one read. Another said simply, "Psalm 3:5." Another declared, "Share with study group!"

It was a gift to have this peek into Annie's heart. But his own heart skipped a beat when he saw his name in the wide margin. "Read this section to Art."

Had she? Annie was always reading him little snippets, but he didn't remember this one. Then again, he had probably been too busy chewing her out for marking in the book. He read the short paragraphs she'd indicated, then scratched his head, uncertain what she'd intended him to glean from the words. Turning to the cover flap, he read the synopsis of the book, trying to put the passage Annie had marked into context.

It was a historical novel set during the Civil War. Art felt his gut twist when he read that the heroine was dying of consumption. No wonder Annie had identified with the story line. He read the paragraphs again.

> Maizie came in and flung open the window, muttering something about fresh air. A minute later, the servant sashayed out of the room with the washbasin sloshing in her ample arms, leaving the scent of lavender in its wake. Sarah

watched from the bed, her thin fingers worrying the rough hem of the coverlet. Maizie had not so much as glanced her way. Sarah wondered if she'd become invisible in her confinement.

Her gaze traveled to the window, and suddenly it was as though she'd been transported beyond the splintered sash. Her sickroom faded to nothing, and she felt as though she were dancing among the willows that bent in the April breeze. She could feel the cool grasses between her bare toes, relish the warmth of the sun on her arms. For one moment, she remembered what it had been like to be healthy and whole. It was a gift. And even as her spirit danced, she thanked the Giver.

Art wondered if Annie had experienced something similar during her illness. He would show this to Maddie and ask her if she understood what Annie might have wanted him to learn from it.

Paging through the last half of the book, he scanned Annie's writings. A notation on the last page was printed in bold letters and underlined twice. It said: "I LOVE this author!"

A soft smile curved Art's lips, and he turned his eyes heavenward. Amazing. After reading the words that contained the essence of all Madeleine Houser was—her heart, her soul, her faith in God—Annie had come to love Maddie. It struck him that perhaps *this* was the message he most needed to hear right now.

He turned to the author's photograph again and brought it slowly to his lips. He was finally ready to let go. And he could hardly wait to tell Maddie.

fourteen

The faux granite countertops were elegant, and Maddie's good china gleamed behind the glass fronts of her new cabinets. She walked across the pristine tiled floor to stand in the doorway and survey the results of weeks of chaos and hard labor. It was finally finished. And it was beautiful. Though Kate had picked out the patterns and colors, Maddie and her sister shared the same taste, and the kitchen really was lovely.

Her days would finally belong to her again. No more letting in a crew of grimy, noisy workmen every morning. No more tripping over sawhorses and stacks of tile every evening. No more microwaved suppers. No more hauling her entire office back and forth each day. The house was livable, and she could finally set up a permanent desk in the empty dining room and finish her book in peace.

So why did she feel so melancholy?

It was a stupid question. She knew why. She would go to the inn for the last time today. She would sit at the smooth oak table and listen to the familiar, soothing creaks and ticks of the old house. She would write her chapters and coax Alex to warm her feet. She would jot down one last note of thanks to Art Tyler. And then she would come home.

Home. The very word made her ache. As beautiful as it was, Kate's fancy house with its new kitchen and spacious rooms had never felt like home. Even the New York loft she'd loved couldn't hold a candle to the one place that had worked its way into her heart. In the space of a few short weeks, Annabeth's Inn had become home to Maddie.

It wasn't the bricks and boards or the cottonwoods and rosebushes—or even the lovable cat—that made it feel like home. It was Art. And knowing that, she wasn't sure she could ever really be at home again.

Sighing heavily, she went to gather her things. She loaded the car and backed out of the driveway. Today, the short drive to the inn felt like a walk to the gallows; every landmark along the way took on new significance, every mile felt ripe with poignancy.

She turned onto Hampton Road and a few minutes later was turning the key in the front door of the inn. She walked through the hall to the dining room. As always, Art's note was waiting—a short one today, she noticed. She wondered what it would say. Had he even remembered that this was her last day? *He's probably celebrating the milestone,* she thought wryly.

She set up her computer and started the coffee, putting

off the moment when she would read Art's final note. When she finally picked it up, his salutation startled her.

Dearest Maddie,

Today is supposed to be your final day at the inn. I know you have a book to finish and I know your deadline is tight, but could I bring lunch at noon and steal a few minutes of your time? There's something I'd like to talk to you about. (If you can't spare the time, I understand. Just leave a message on my cell phone.)

Happy writing,
Art

She turned the note over, hoping to find a postscript that would offer a clue to what he wanted to talk to her about. But the page was blank. How did he expect her to concentrate, knowing that he would be walking through the door in a few hours?

She went into the rest room off the main-floor bedroom and inspected her reflection. Had she known he would be here, she would have done something with her hair this morning besides gather it into a loose ponytail. And she might have chosen something to wear besides this comfy wind suit—although the jewel-toned pattern did bring out the color of her eyes. She wasn't accustomed to dressing up for work. Well, he'd just have to suffer looking at her messy dishwater hair and casual attire.

She barely managed to write a thousand words before the clock struck twelve. Right on schedule, she heard the key in the door to the apartment below. She moistened her lips, quickly saved her file, and put her computer in sleep mode.

Footsteps sounded on the steps, and Maddie went to the head of the stairs. Art was balancing two round plastic containers in his hands and attempting to secure two large paper cups with his chin, while the cat wove his way back and forth between Art's feet.

She hurried down the steps and met him halfway. "Here, let me take some of this. Alex, go on now. Mmmm. . .smells good. What are we having?"

Art grinned and winked at her. "Chicken noodle soup. I'm told it's good for what ails you." He transferred the warm containers to her hands.

She returned his smile but felt a little miffed at him. Why did he always have to come off as though he were flirting with her? If he didn't have room in his heart for another woman, why did he turn on the charm with her?

She took the soup into the kitchen and transferred it into thick, pottery bowls. Enticing aromas filled the room. "Is this from the deli?" she called out to the dining room, where she heard him scooting chairs around. The drinks had borne the deli's label, but their takeout usually came in Styrofoam containers.

He came and stood in the doorway between the two

rooms and watched while she fixed a tray with crackers and spoons. "The drinks are from the deli. Actually, Ginny made the soup for us."

"Really?" That was interesting. Ginny had been over the night before to borrow the newspaper. She hadn't mentioned anything about soup.

Maddie swept past Art, carrying the tray out to the table. Art put folded napkins at each place and removed the lids from their drinks. Now he came and held her chair for her.

"Thank you, Sir."

He took the chair to her left and spread a napkin on his lap. "Shall we bless the food?"

Maddie nodded and bowed her head.

Art cleared his throat, then surprised her by reaching for her hand. His grasp was warm and firm—and rather unsettling.

"Father God, we thank You for this day and for this food. Please bless our time together, and especially bless the dear hands that prepared this food. In Jesus' name, amen."

He squeezed Maddie's hand before he let it go.

They ate in silence for a few minutes, then Art wiped his mouth and pushed back from the table. "Maddie, I want to talk to you about something."

She swallowed a bite of soup and put down her spoon. "Okay. . . ."

Art bent his head and rubbed circles in the smooth finish of the table with his fingertips. "I owe you an apology.

You. . .well, you took me by surprise that day I first realized who you were. Before I'd had time to think about the consequences, I'd already asked you for a date. That wasn't fair to you."

Maddie's defenses went up. Here it came—the big breakup scene that was all too familiar. Never fear, though; she had her lines memorized.

Meanwhile, Art dutifully continued delivering his own lines. "The truth is, I was a very confused man. I wasn't looking for another relationship because. . .well, I guess I'd known true love, and I didn't believe I could ever find that with anyone else."

From the edge of her consciousness, Maddie became aware that Art was speaking in the past tense. She started paying attention.

"For awhile, grief crippled me," he went on. "But I've been talking to some very wise counselors recently, and I do believe they've brought me to my senses."

"C–counselors?" She waited for him to expound.

With one easy motion, Art moved his chair closer to hers and enveloped her right hand in both of his. "Maddie, I don't want to rush you, but I don't want to let you get away, either. When you told me that your house was finished and that you wouldn't be coming out here to write anymore, it. . ." He shook his head and swallowed hard. "I don't know. It scared me. I know it sounds crazy because it's not like we were ever here together. But I liked coming home to find your notes. They were the highlight of my day, and I'll miss them like crazy. I liked walking up the stairs and catching the faintest scent of your perfume. And that day I was home sick. . . Oh, Maddie, you can't imagine how wonderful it was to hear your laughter up here. I don't want to lose that."

Though her backside was firmly planted on the brocade pad of her chair, Maddie felt some part of her rise up and begin to soar.

Alex sauntered to the table, tail held high, and situated himself between them. The cat looked from Maddie to Art and back again, then pushed his weight hard against Maddie's leg, begging to be petted.

Art gave him a gentle shove with the side of his foot. "Go on, Alex. Come on, Buddy. You're cramping my style here."

Alex plopped down on top of Maddie's feet. Art ignored him and scooted his chair another inch closer. "What I'm trying to say is that I know now that it's very possible I may find love again. And I'm ready to embrace the possibility."

She sat speechless as one hot tear escaped and rolled down her cheek.

Art let go of her hand. He reached up to thread his fingers through her hair and smudged the tear away with his thumb. "Oh, Maddie, I'm so sorry I hurt you. Could we. . .begin again?"

She nodded, her heart as full as her throat.

Art stroked her hair away from her temple and looked

into her eyes. "I–I desperately want to kiss you right now. Would that be all right?"

In an instant, she was in his arms, and then he was kissing her forehead, her temples, his lips brushing away the tears of joy that streaked her cheeks. Finally, gently, he matched his lips to hers.

When he drew away, they were both breathless.

"Wow," Maddie said, drawing the word out.

"Yeah, wow," he echoed, kissing her again. He brushed a strand of hair off her face, then cupped the palm of his hand around her cheek. "I have so much I want to tell you. God has done some pretty neat things in my life these past few days."

"Really?"

He nodded. "You may be the writer, but I have some stories of my own to tell."

She reached up and put her hand over his, savoring the warmth of his skin. "I can't wait to hear your stories, Art."

That familiar spark flared in his smoky eyes. "What if I told you that you were the heroine in some of them?"

She flashed him a grin. "I'd say turnabout is fair play."

Their mingled laughter rang through the house.